# Burying Pinkie Pie

a novel by

David Sparks

To Judy (HANNAH)
you know this

Copyright © 2017 by David Sparks. All rights reserved. No part of this book may be reproduced or transmitted in any form or by any means without permission in writing from the author.

I want to thank Mason McCann Smith, my editor and a whole lot more on this book. For my second straight book I can say, if it weren't for Mason, this would not have been written. He's a good man.

I owe particular thanks to Vicki Hurst and the other ladies in the tennis shop at the Pass Club in Boca Grande. They read drafts, commented, and encouraged. My daughter Grace did the same.

Because it's a challenge to write in the voice of a seventeen-year-old boy, I recruited a number of teenagers to read portions of the book and give me feedback. My teacher cousin, Nancy Graham, recruited some of her students. This was invaluable. Thanks to everyone.

I also want to thank my wife, Julie DiNapoli Sparks, for giving me the time and resources to write, plus the opportunity to get acquainted with the real Pinkie Pie.

Finally, thanks to all the people who keep the spirit and history of the Calusa Indian tribe alive.

Cover art by Brendan Coudal, Ballyhoo Designs.
www.BrendanCoudal.com

Dedicated to my wife

Julie DiNapoli Sparks

# Introduction

My name is Wendell Wolf.

This was supposed to be my creative writing class senior project, a 25-page short story. But when I got done with my short story, I realized I hadn't told the *whole* story. So my English teacher, Mr. Sanders (who is a good guy for a teacher (just kidding, Mr. Sanders)) told me he would count it as my project even if it was longer. So it turned out to be a really long paper, and I guess now it's more like a book. Mr. Sanders also said he'd keep it a secret until after I graduated. Which was good, because there's stuff in the story which I don't want people to know, because I'd like to get out of Banyan Island High School without people thinking I'm some sort of psycho.

There are a couple of things I need to mention before you read this book.

First, the "f-bombs." Mr. Sanders counted 28 f-bombs in my first draft of this story. Well, I'm not going to say anything about the kind of teacher who counts his student's f-bombs. That worked out to around one f-bomb for every seven pages, which didn't seem like that many to me, but to Mr. Sanders it was 28 too many.

Mr. Sanders said the f-bomb is a cheap, lazy word. He says it was like I couldn't be bothered to come up with a different word that actually means something.

I told him, "It's a real word, Mr. Sanders. Everybody uses it these days, and everybody knows exactly what it means."

He gave me that look of his over the top of his glasses. That look just kept boring into me, and his forehead got this furrow in it, and his eyebrows started twitching, and his thin little lips got kind of tense, and he reached up and gave the end of his mustache a couple of tugs like he always does when he's annoyed at me, and he said, "Not in my class they don't."

So, okay, I mentioned I wanted to get out of high school, right? So we compromised. No actual f-bombs. You'll see what I mean.

And here's another thing. When my dad found out I wrote this book, he told me I had to start it with the letter he made me write to him after all this stuff happened. Like it wasn't enough to apologize to him, I had to let all his friends know I was saying *Sorry*, too. Kind of weird, huh? Well, I admit I put him through a lot. So, here it is:

**Dear Joel (I call my dad Joel),**

I met with Sheriff Pruitt to discuss the "consequences of my actions." According to Sheriff Pruitt, the following are crimes (according to Florida State Law) that I might have committed.

1. Simple assault. Causing someone to fall down in pig shit. I don't think I did this, she just slipped.
2. Theft by unauthorized taking. "Borrowing" your Escalade. Did it.
3. Theft. Taking the money from your golf bag. I don't have any excuse for this one.
4. Destruction of property. The dead pig smell in your car. The Sheriff said this is an "iffy" one. Basically, it's a crime if the smell is really bad and stays a long time.
5. Theft. A dead animal. This is definitely a crime, especially if someone (Officer Hultz) wanted to press charges. Sheriff Pruitt didn't know whether this was a misdemeanor or a felony because no one can figure out the price of a dead pig.
6. Theft. The unauthorized use of a cherry picker. This might be considered theft, but I don't think it was because I paid for it.
7. Aiding and abetting a theft. The Sheriff's boat. Technically, this was Reggie, but I went along.
8. Disturbing a marine sanctuary. Dead pig in Manatee Hole. This is a federal crime, but I don't think we disturbed anything.
9. Theft. One used shirt, Banyan Bargains. I did it.
10. Animal cruelty. Putting Pepe the Chihuahua and the rooster in the drainage pipe. I did it, but I think they both had fun in there with the alligator.
11. Making a false 911 call. In my opinion, that *was* a situation where people's lives could have been in danger. (The alligator)

12. Assault. My hand and the back of your head. Did it. (Sorry)
13. Theft. A dead animal, second time. (See 5)
14. Destruction of property. Digging under the Big Banyan. Technically, this was Jordan Minch, but Sheriff Pruitt said he was doing it under my supervision.
15. Illegal disposal of a dead animal. I'm sorry, but I still don't think this was a crime.

Sincerely,

Wendell Wolf

## Pinkie Pie Gets Run Over

A good place to start this story is the day Pinkie Pie was killed. Pinkie belonged to Samantha Granger, who liked to be called Sam. Sam's pretty much been my best (and only) friend since I moved here last year.

Sam's family ran a marina on the island called — wait for it — Granger's. There was another marina on the island, but it was more a place where the winter people docked their yachts, gassed up and ate at a fancy restaurant. Granger's Marina was totally different than that. They sold bait and fishing supplies, pumped gas, worked on boats, and Sam kept a bunch of animals: sheep, goats, a giant rabbit, a three-legged dog named Tripod, a blind beagle named Bailey, and until this all happened, a huge pink pig called Pinkie Pie.

Sam's mom (Mandy Granger) was supposed to be in charge, but she always had a hangover and mostly she just sat in her trailer all day watching game shows and soap operas on television. Sam always said she didn't know where her dad was and that's an important part of this story.

Back to Pinkie Pie. Sam did nearly all the work around the marina, including feeding all the animals in the morning before school. Pinkie Pie lived in a pen made of wobbly wooden stakes and chicken wire, and two or three mornings a week, she'd just trample the chicken wire and wander off into the neighborhood. Since I lived across the street from Granger's, I'd usually see Sam out searching, and I'd hurry outside to help. Pinkie was a gigantic pig, she came up my waist, but I'm sort of short. OK, I'm pretty short. OK, I'm short. Still, she had to be one of the biggest pigs around. Plus she was pink and she had a white star in the middle of her forehead. So, she was always easy to find.

That Thursday morning we hunted for Pinkie along Shore Road just down the street from the marina. Sam called for her and rattled some rabbit food in a can to get her to come. I don't know why we ever did that, because we always found Pinkie digging in some neighbor's yard looking for roots. It always seemed to me that the pig liked roots more than the rabbit food.

I was on the other side of the street from Sam, looking in a neighbor's goldfish pond. We found Pinkie in there once, wallowing around, cooling off. The neighbor wasn't very happy about it, but Sam bought him off with some smoked mullet.

Everyone on Banyan Island drove golf carts. Most of the fishing guides drove big pick-ups with their gear in the back and the winter people had their convertibles, but everyone had a golf cart. Most of the carts were electric and you could barely hear them coming because they made a low, whirring noise. But, some of the winter people had gotten these tricked out gas-fueled carts with big, knobby tires. These carts were faster and they made a lot more noise—but not, I guess, loud enough for Pinkie Pie to hear.

Sam and I heard the golf cart coming, but we couldn't see it. Shore Road made a sharp turn around a huge palm tree and the cart was on the other side of the turn. We heard the screech of rubber on pavement, a terrible thump, a crash and then a lot of screaming. Some of the screaming was human, I could tell, and some of it was awful, sounds I'd never heard before.

I looked at Sam and she looked back. Her black eyes were huge. "Shit" was all she said. We both knew what had just happened.

The golf cart was on its side under the palm. I don't know why, but I remember it had one of those sparkle paint jobs and one of its front wheels was still spinning. Gas leaked out onto the pavement. There were two people on the ground next to the cart, a woman and a kid my age. I recognized the kid. Ethan Pugsley was part of the "Lax Bros" at school, mostly the kids who played lacrosse or maybe didn't play lacrosse, but they dressed like it. (My favorite, Nike sandals with black Nike socks. Have you ever tried to wear socks with sandals? It's stupid, especially when there's a lot of sand around and we live on a stupid island in Florida—duh.)

The woman was his mom, Mrs. Pugsley. Of all the people on the island to run over Pinkie, she was the worst. I'll get to that later. She always drove too fast on the days Ethan was too late for school to use his skateboard. She sat in the street, sobbing, and Ethan was holding his arm, screaming.

Pinkie Pie was a real mess. It was pretty obvious she'd been hit by the cart. She was on her back in the middle of the road kicking all four legs in the air. She shook her head back and forth and every time she shook, the blood sprayed around like it was coming from a sprinkler. Even grosser, she shit all over the road. The shit and blood mixed with the gas leaking from the cart made the road really slippery. And it stunk.

I couldn't believe the noise Pinkie made. It was an unbelievable sound—a hoarse, low moan going up into a high scream, again and again—louder than anything I'd ever heard.

What happened next was kind a blur, but I pieced it together afterwards. Sam moved to take care of Pinkie, but she had to avoid Pinkie's sharp hooves whirling around in the air. The big pig tried to get up, but her two back legs were broken. I saw the bones pushing through her skin.

Ethan sat right in the middle of all the mess on the street, screaming and holding his arm. Mrs. Pugsley stood up and shouted at Sam. There was a siren coming from the middle of town and people came out of their houses and they ran toward us. I remember a couple of them were on their phones and one asshat was actually taking pictures. I focused on the first group. Sam's mom was in the lead. She was wearing her regular outfit, a Tampa Bay jersey and camo pajama pants. As usual she had a cigarette in her mouth.

At this point, everything happened in slow motion, at least in my memory. Maybe it's because I was asked about it so many times. Officer Hultz arrived in the Animal Control golf cart. That's where the siren came from. I went over and knelt down next to Sam and Pinkie Pie. Pinkie stopped kicking, and she just lay there in the street, panting really heavy. Sam was crying and holding Pinkie's head. Pinkie's blood was splattered on Sam's face.

Officer Hultz pulled Sam away from Pinkie. Mrs. Pugsley shoved herself between Officer Hultz and Sam, and she shouted. "You stupid bitch! Why can't you keep that frigging pig tied up?" Officer Hultz went back to her golf cart and came back with her gun. Hultz was all the time stopping by the marina threatening Sam because she had too many animals. Hultz always said she was going to do something about it. I guess this was her chance.

"No!" Sam screamed.

Then, "Smack!" It wasn't really a huge noise, it sounded like someone slapped a fat piece of meat. There was a smoky firecracker smell in the air. Pinkie stopped squirming around in the street and there was a little bloody hole in the front of her head, right through the white star.

I looked over at Sam and her face was frozen. Her regular dark skin was now real white and the pig blood on it made her look like she was wearing a Halloween mask. The tears on her cheeks made little streams through the blood. I knew right away this wasn't going to be good. Pinkie Pie was much more than a regular pig to Sam Granger.

"Arrest her," Mrs. Pugsley yelled at Officer Hultz, who had a weird smile on her face. Hultz seemed pleased that she'd just killed Pinkie. She just shrugged and stood there. Shooting Pinkie probably was a big enough deal to Hultz. She didn't need to arrest anybody to make her day better.

Sam bowed her head and knelt in the street. She whispered in Pinkie's dead ear. I heard the word "Nokoomis."

"You people are trash." I remember this part clearly. Mrs. Pugsley was so pissed that spit came out of her mouth. She leaned down and grabbed the string of shells Sam always wore around her neck. "Are you listening to me?"

Sam's head jerked back when Mrs. Pugsley pulled on her necklace.

"Are you listening to me?" She whispered it this time, like an evil witch.

That's when it happened. I saw red and then a flash. I reached over and grabbed Mrs. Pugsley's hand to pull it off Sam's necklace. Right then, the necklace broke and Sam's special olive shells spilled all over the road. When the necklace broke, Mrs. Pugsley fell in the street, right next to Ethan, right in the blood-gas-pig shit mixture. She wore a white tennis dress that flipped up and I could see her underwear. I didn't want to look, but I did. Her underwear was yellow.

She rolled around, screaming. "You son a bitch. You pushed me." She wasn't hurt, I could tell. She was more surprised, plus, she probably ruined her tennis dress falling in the crap on the street. But I didn't push her.

That's pretty much how the whole thing started.

## We Meet With Officer Hultz and Sheriff Pruitt

I'm adopted, and I don't know what name I had when I was born, but I was named "Wendell" by my adopted parents, Joel and Bunny Wolf. I know I was born in Russia, so I was probably named Sergei or Igor or something, any of which would have been better than Wendell.

I was adopted as a baby. It was a fad then, because I know a lot of my parents' friends adopted kids from Russia. I can't ever forget I was adopted from Russia, because whenever I do something wrong, I hear about how it's because I'm from Russia. People used to whisper about it when I was little. Now they just talk about it like it's a fact.

I grew up in Connecticut, but a year ago my parents moved to Banyan Island. It's an island, but it's connected to the mainland by a bridge. The rich people don't like the bridge because it lets regular people visit.

I suppose Banyan Island is a nice place, especially if you're rich. It's ten miles long with beaches all over the place. The water is blue and clear, and people who live here spend all their time fishing and playing tennis and golf. That's for the rich people. (They're called "winter people.") Everyone else works. (They're called "islanders.")

Lots of tourists visit the island, and there are three things they always do:

1. Stop at Granger's because it is so "quaint."
2. Look at the giant Banyan trees.
3. Take pictures of the island's alligator. There's just one alligator on the island, and he lives in a drainage pipe right near the school. On sunny days, he comes out of the pipe and hangs out on the grass next to the ditch that goes into the pipe. Nobody except Officer Hultz thinks he's dangerous, but the people at the Banyan Inn told her not to mess with it because the guests at the Inn like it.

The whole town revolves around this old hotel called the Banyan Inn. Somebody decided the Banyan Inn should have a bunch of condos, and Joel bought one and now he kind of works for the Inn, selling condos to other people. This mainly means Joel plays golf every day, supposedly getting people to buy condos.

If you ask my mom, she'll say we moved here because I needed a "fresh start."

It seems like I've always been in trouble. I just can't stop saying or doing what I think. The counselors call it "impulsivity." I'm working on it, though I still get in trouble.

The earliest memory I have is that thing with the dog and Greggy. I was playing at a house down the street with a kid named Greggy and a girl named Peggy. We were taking turns holding Peggy's beagle, Echo. Greggy thought it was funny to make Echo growl by squeezing its foot. I was holding Echo, Greggy reached over to grab his foot. I saw red and I bit him on the arm. It turns out, it wasn't just a little bite, it cut something in there and made him really bleed. He ran off crying, and I just sat there with Peggy holding Echo. I knew I was in trouble. Right after that, Greggy's mom came running across the yard holding Greggy against her huge chest and she was screaming at me, waving his bloody arm around.

My mom and dad took me to meet with Greggy's parents, and I had to apologize while Greggy just stood there. I heard whispered words—"Russian," "genetics," and then other words I didn't understand—"fetal alcohol syndrome."

Greggy's parents never let him play with me again, although I think he wanted to. I think I was about five when that happened and I was in kindergarten. That's when I remember meeting with my first counselor at school. At the time it didn't seem like any big thing. Bite a kid, see a counselor. What did I know?

It was Friday, the day after Pinkie was killed, and instead of going to school, we were all sitting in this small patio room in the back of the library. It's not really a room, it's sort of a porch, open on all sides so you can see the flower gardens and fountains. There wasn't a police station on the island, which was probably why we were there.

Officer Hultz was at the front table, and she had Sheriff Pruitt with her. Sheriff Pruitt was actually a deputy sheriff, but everybody called him "Sheriff." He only came onto the island once in a while. Most of the time he patrolled the mainland. Everybody on the island liked Sheriff Pruitt. He was a pretty good guy who drove around in a big SUV. When big stuff happened, he showed up. I guess Mrs. Pugsley crashing into Pinkie Pie was big stuff.

Pruitt and Hultz were both in their uniforms. Pruitt's gun belt creaked when he moved around in his chair. Hultz's uniform shirt was too tight, and in the front you could see rolls of fat under it. She was wearing a badge with little bars hanging on a chain from it. Probably her iguana kill-count.

Twenty years ago, Banyan Island was over-run by iguanas. Iguanas weren't native to the island or even to Florida, but some asshat had them as pets, they escaped, supposedly they breed faster than rabbits (look it up), and voila!—now, we've got a problem. There was iguana shit everywhere. When the winter ladies came out of their doors in the morning to walk their little yapping dogs, they'd see a three-foot iguana (big lizard) staring at them from a palm tree. And, speaking of little dogs, the rumor was that iguanas ate people's pets. I don't believe it, because it was hard to imagine a lizard getting its mouth around a cat or a dog, and besides, I think they only eat vegetables.

The winter people hated the iguanas. When the winter people don't like something, then shit starts to happen. The Town Council started up the Banyan Island Animal Control. They hired a crazy lady named Officer Hultz. Nobody knew her first name. She just made everybody call her Officer Hultz. Nobody ever knew where she came from, but the rumor was she was a prison guard in New York and got injured in a knife attack during a riot. If it was a knife attack, it must have been a pretty big knife, because Officer Hultz was huge. She filled most of the seat of her golf cart, and it was built for two people.

Somehow Officer Hultz also got put in charge of security at the Banyan Inn. Since everything in town revolved around the Inn, Officer Hultz was a pain in everybody's ass.

A bunch of us were in chairs facing Officer Hultz and Sheriff Pruitt.

My mom and Joel, me, Sam and her mom, Mrs. Pugsley and Ethan. Ethan had a big sling on his right arm. What a titty-baby (Sam's favorite expression).

OK, about why it was bad news that it was Mrs. Pugsley who hit Pinkie: Mrs. Pugsley is married to Stephen Pugsley. He's the general manager of the Inn. That made him Joel's (my dad's) boss.

I can understand people sucking up to their boss, but Joel's a rock star at sucking up. At home, it was "Pugsley said this" and "Pugsley did that." I mean, it was nauseating. Joel's a grown man. He's too old for a man-crush. But, if it were biologically possible, Joel would have Pugsley's baby (I know, gross thought).

As long as I'm explaining about Pugsley and Joel, here's some other bad news. The people at the Inn (Pugsley, Joel, and the other asshats over there) would have liked to bulldoze Granger's and build a bunch of condos. Plus, the marina's some kind of historic site since it's been there for way over a hundred years, and Pugsley was pissed they get a big break on their taxes. Believe me, I knew all about this. Joel was always looking out the window at the marina, making hissing noises.

So, the golf cart belonged to the Pugsleys, the hurt kid was Ethan Pugsley, the messed up dress belonged to Mrs. Pugsley, the dead pig (and Sam) came from the marina that was a constant irritation to the Pugsleys, like an eyelash that gets loose under your eyelid. Plus, Pugsley was Officer Hultz's boss, too. Got all that?

Things didn't look good.

Joel was dressed in his usual golf clothes. First thing every morning, he put on some weird color pants and a Banyan Inn golf shirt. That day he looked bored. My mom was doing her yoga thing with her stupid black tights and *Flashdance* sweatshirt.

Officer Hultz started off. "We're here today to discuss yesterday's golf cart/pig incident."

I felt a little queasy when I heard her call it an "incident." I don't know what I'd call it, but "incident" sounded too official.

I heard shuffling from behind us. Someone else was coming in the room. When I looked around, I saw it was my counselor from the high school, Ms. Gordon. I looked at my mother, who just shrugged and then fired a look back at me. I knew what the look meant. "You screwed up again. You'll always have counselors."

Ms. Gordon sat down behind us. I could tell she was wearing her stupid flowery perfume. I had to put up with that smell for an hour every Wednesday morning.

Officer Hultz started again. "The pig/golf cart incident?" She said it like a question.

One by one, we had to tell our side of the story. Mrs. Pugsley started and told her story and after that she kept interrupting other people until Sheriff Pruitt had to tell her to settle down. But he was nice. The Sheriff had a southern accent and southerners never seem concerned about anything. Except football.

Sam was next, and except for the fact that she was dressed in her most outrageous Calusa Indian outfit, I thought she did a good job explaining what happened. She was wearing another shell necklace, just like every day I'd ever known her. She also had on this leather vest thing that had a big sea turtle embroidered on the back. Sam looked better than her mother, though. Her mom wore a Dolphins jersey, flowered pajama pants, and slippers. You could see her cigarettes in the pocket of her pants.

Then it was my turn, and I tried to start at the beginning, but what they all wanted to talk about was me "pushing" Mrs. Pugsley. Nobody was really interested in what happened to Pinkie Pie except Sam, and what could she do? Pinkie Pie was dead. It didn't matter that Mrs. Pugsley was speeding and Pinkie Pie was an innocent pig.

Sheriff Pruitt asked, "Wendell, what were you thinking when you pushed Mrs. Pugsley?"

I started to get pissed, then I took a breath and counted to five. I thought I had explained it already. "I didn't really think. I had hold of Sam's necklace and it broke, and Mrs. Pugsley also had a hold on it, and when it broke, she fell down. There was no pushing."

Off to the side I heard Mrs. Pugsley snort and whisper something.

I think it was "liar."

Someone cleared their throat behind me. "Sheriff Pruitt?" My heart sank. It was my mother. Things never got better when my mother talked. Pruitt looked up and nodded.

"Sheriff, I think you should know some of the challenges Wendell has faced. I asked his counselor from school, Ms. Gordon, to attend this meeting and speak to these points."

Ms. Gordon always wore a pair of reading glasses on a string around her neck. From there, the glasses sat on her enormous boobs like they were on a shelf. Before she spoke, Ms. Gordon always made a big deal out of putting those glasses on. I had to sit through it every Wednesday morning. After the glasses, she opened a file on her lap.

She cleared her throat and looked up. "Thank you, Sheriff. At the outset, I'd like to say, I have permission from Wendell's parents to reveal some of his background."

I looked up at my mother, and she shrugged. Joel looked away toward the fountain. I couldn't believe we were going to sit here while Ms. Gordon told them stuff from my file.

"Uh," I decided to speak up, but I couldn't figure out what to say. "Uh." I looked at Ms. Gordon, because I didn't know who else to look at. "Can you do that?"

Ms. Gordon gave me one of her "I'm here for you" looks and "you're an idiot" at the same time. "Florida law specifies that parents have authority over minors' mental health records until the age of eighteen."

Of course, everybody in the room knew I was only seventeen. Officer Hultz had announced it at the beginning of the meeting. But I already knew that my mind was focused on something else. *Mental health records? Is that what she was calling my file? And she was going to read it?* I thought about all the stuff Ms. Gordon and I had talked about. I mean, she'd been my counselor since I started at Banyan Island High School the year before.

Then I focused on what Ms. Gordon was saying. She'd already launched into her speech. "...adopted as a baby from Russia...possible fetal alcohol syndrome...early behavior problems...impulse control."

Fudging Russian stuff again. My mind strayed, and then I came back when I heard her say "an incident with a neighbor child." The biting thing again. I'd talked to Ms. Gordon about this maybe a hundred times. For some reason, she was fascinated by it, and she kept bringing it up. How many times in my life did she expect me to bite another kid? It wasn't like I was Hannibal Lecter.

"When the neighbor child reached across Wendell to retrieve his pet, Wendell bit him on the wrist, inflicting a significant laceration and causing substantial bleeding."

Then she stopped like that was it. What she didn't say was that Greggy was hurting Echo, I got mad, and now I hate it when people yell at me. That's the whole story.

"Wendell has struggled in school maintaining the pace of his peers, in all likelihood due to attention deficit and impulse control issues, which are commonly found in Russian adoptees."

I looked around. Everybody was listening. *Does Ms. Gordon really need to read this shit in front of all these people?* I looked over at my mother—not that she'd do anything to stop it. I glanced at Mrs. Pugsley who was staring at me like I was some kind of demented lab animal.

"This lack of progress in school is no doubt the prime contributor to Wendell's poor verbal skills. When he was younger, he was more verbal, but now he has a harder time expressing himself. This has resulted in Wendell having few, if any friends." *How long is this going to go on?*

"A year ago, when Wendell transferred to Banyan Island High, it was our recommendation that he receive on-going counseling in our special education unit. While he hasn't made the progress we would have liked to see in terms of his social skills, he has bonded with Samantha Granger, who lives across the street from the Wolfs. As you know, it was Samantha's pig who was killed in the unfortunate incident."

OK, there it was. Ms. Gordon dropped the big one. The special education unit, AKA, the Sped Shed. A big white doublewide trailer next to the high school where all the kids went when nobody could figure out what to do with them. It's where I saw Ms. Gordon.

Over on her side of the room, Mrs. Pugsley nodded. Everybody in town knew about the Sped Shed. You might as well call me an ax murderer.

I love those prison shows on television, mainly because they remind me of high school, except we have fewer gang tattoos and shaved heads (and murderers, probably). Just like in prison, we've got our high school gangs—the skaters, the lax bros, the DQ's (drama queens), nerds, and even a couple of goths.

And then there's the Sped Shed. While other kids drift in and out of their gangs, when you go the Sped Shed, it pretty much stays with you for life. The Sped Shed might as well have had a big neon sign out front: "Loser Headquarters." Even though I only went there to see Ms. Gordon, I got the label: a Sped Shed kid.

Sheriff Pruitt cleared his throat and pulled his papers together. "I think we've heard enough."

It was pretty clear it was decided beforehand. Gordon, Hultz, and Pruitt must have talked. What do you do when a Sped Shed kid screws up? More time in the Sped Shed. I mean, it's a Sped Shed kid, right? They can't really get in trouble, it's not their fault. The verdict? I ended up sentenced to another hour of counseling a week with Ms. Gordon for the rest of the year. Mrs. Pugsley wasn't happy about it, but what did she want them to do, waterboard me?

Sheriff Pruitt thought the meeting was over. He stood up, adjusted his gun belt, and said something to Officer Hultz.

Sam shot to her feet. "What about Pinkie Pie?"

For some reason, Pruitt smiled at Sam. He looked at Officer Hultz, who was having a hard time dragging her big butt out from between the arms of the plastic chair. It was obvious he wanted Hultz to answer.

"The pig is dead." She grunted it out as she bent over with the chair on her ass. There was a silence after that. Everyone there was like (sorry Mr. Sanders, I promised I wouldn't say "like") "No shit. Tell us something we didn't know."

"Where is she?" Sam's voice was a little louder.

Officer Hultz sat back down cleared her throat. "Um…the pig's… remains…are in storage as evidence pending this…hearing."

Sam spoke up. "I need Pinkie Pie back."

Officer Hultz looked confused. Everybody else had started to leave, and they sat back down. Behind me, I heard my father say something to my mother about his "goddam tee time."

Officer Hultz looked over at Sheriff Pruitt, who just shrugged. She pulled her words together. "It's…the policy of the Animal Control Office to… dispose…"—you could tell she was trying to say the right thing—"…of animal…carcasses…in an approved…and responsible manner." There, she got it out. She looked over at Sam with a cruel little smile.

"Where is Pinkie?" Sam was pretty calm, but you could tell she was getting pissed. Sam didn't get pissed very often, but when she did… watch out!

"The pig's remains are stored at the Animal Shelter prior to disposal."

Everyone knew where the Animal Shelter was, on the mainland next to the sewerage plant. The whole place was huge, and it really smelled along that stretch of road. A lot of the winter ladies volunteered at the shelter. They wouldn't have the kind of dog they saw at the shelter as their own pet, but they didn't mind taking care of them.

"What do you mean, Pinkie is being 'stored'?"

I was impressed by Sam. She really wanted answers to her questions.

Then Officer Hultz sighed, and her voice sounded like she was talking to a little kid. "When animals' remains are received at the shelter, they are stored until there is an adequate amount…of…volume for a bulk cremation. The remains are kept in a freezer until that event."

There was a silence in the room, and you could tell everyone was thinking the same thing. Pinkie Pie was a huge pig. The Animal Shelter must have a freezer as big as the North Pole.

"I need Pinkie Pie back. My grandmother's spirit lives in Pinkie Pie." Sam said it, and she just stood there.

That shut everybody up.

# Understanding Sam Granger

To understand this story, you need to know about Sam Granger.

Banyan Island's like a big park, everything's all clean and washed and mowed. A hundred years ago, rich people started coming down because the fishing was good, and some of them got the idea of spiffing the place up. So, they built the Inn and a golf course, and they even put in a place where they all dress in white and play croquet on special grass.

Banyan Island is on the Gulf of Mexico but there are canals running all through it that people live on so they can have boats. There is one big canal running through the island and that's called the bayou.

When you come into town, there's one house where the hedge grows right through holes cut in a stone wall and they have guys trim the hedge so it's nice and flat. There's one whole street that's a tunnel under huge Banyan trees. There's a used clothes store in the middle of town where the rich people donate their stuff – stuff like they probably wore once or twice – and other rich people buy it. There's one house where a bunch of Cuban guys come in the morning and rake the gravel in their driveway. Seriously, I'm not making this shit up.

So, the day we moved here, the moving van pulled away and I sat in my bedroom on the second floor of our new condo, looking across the street at the marina. I was really amazed by the place, so I made a list. (Note to readers: I like to make lists. It makes me feel like I know what I'm doing. One counselor said it was because I had self-esteem issues. Whatever.) Anyway, here's my list:

1. Five boats on trailers, four trailers without boats, three boats without trailers.
2. Two huge pontoons from a pontoon boat, but no boat.
3. A shark cage. (Knew it because I saw it on Discovery)
4. A big truck filled with old refrigerators, washers and dryers.
5. A row of animal cages and stalls, containing (or not containing, because they were running loose) one huge pink pig, two goats, three

white turkey-birds, three dogs, four rabbits, one duck and a llama.

6. A dock running next to an old falling-down building where there was a sign that said they sold "Tackel".

7. Three or four guys scooping fish out of a tank and putting them in buckets.

8. A bunch of machinery, two old trucks, three lawnmowers (in pieces), an ATV, two golf carts, also in pieces.

9. A boat with holes in it that they used as a planter.

10. And a rusty RV where I'm pretty sure people lived.

And this was only what I could see from my window. Seriously.

Right in the middle of the dusty parking lot was this girl, I thought she was a girl, maybe my age, but you couldn't tell because she was so big. I tried to figure out how big she was and it was hard from where I was, but it looked like she was maybe six feet tall. That would make her six or seven inches taller than me. She had on a t-shirt and jean overalls, the kind farmers wore. She had long black hair with two braids going down her back, and she had this big necklace of shells around her neck. I mean, this wasn't a little shell necklace like you saw in tourist stores, these shells were the size of lemons and they were on a leather braid.

And she was dark. Not dark like an African American or a Latino and not dark like really tan, but her skin was this dusty brown color.

I watched her dumping something in a row of bowls on the sand and figured it must be food for the animals. The pig, the dogs, the turkey-birds and the duck were lined up to eat. When the pig leaned down to eat, she squatted down and it looked like she was talking to it. And not only was she talking to it, but every now and then it looked like she was listening to something the pig said. I know it sounds weird, but I watched this carefully and that's what I saw.

Then the girl stood up from the pig and looked right up at me. I was behind a curtain, but I ducked down. How did she know I was there? I sneaked a look back up over the windowsill and she was talking to that pig again. Great. My parents moved us to a new town, and already I'm a stalker. Double great.

The next morning was the first day of my junior year and my first day at Banyan Island High School. I walked out in front of the house in the clothes I wore to school in Connecticut, cargo shorts and a t-shirt. I was pretty nervous about the whole new school thing. The dark animal girl walked toward me across the parking lot of the marina. She was dressed the same as she was the day before, she was going to wear those overalls—I think they were the same overalls—to school. She still had that big necklace on, maybe it was a different one. I wasn't an expert in Calusa Indian necklaces then like I am now.

She walked right up to me and stuck out her hand for a regular handshake, like an adult. I didn't really know what to do, I was used to fist bumps and some guys did bro-hugs, which I hate, probably because I don't have any "bros." I didn't think I had ever shaken hands with a girl. But she had her hand out for a shake. Me not knowing what to do wasn't helped by the fact that standing next to her showed me how huge she was (or what a midget I was; I'm only 5'5").

"I'm Sam Granger."

I didn't say anything at first, I was still sort of in shock by the whole thing. Here was this giant girl I'd been watching holding her hand out to me and she had a boy's name. I shook her hand. Her hand was huge, too, and it was rough. "I'm Wendell Wolf."

"Wendell Wolf." She looked me up and down as she repeated it. "Wendell Wolf." She said it again. I thought she might be getting ready to make fun of my name, but then I decided she was just considering it.

"I watched you feed your animals last night." I decided to start first and get her to think I wasn't spying on her.

She answered right back. "I know. Nokoomis saw you watching." She looked right into my eyes like she was searching for something in there. Her eyes were black—the darkest I'd ever seen.

*Who the hell was this Nokoomis who saw me watching?*

"Nokoomis?" It was all I could think to say. I didn't even know if I was pronouncing it right.

She shifted her book bag to her other shoulder. She had huge muscles in her dark arms. "Nokoomis is the spirit of my grandmother. She lives in Pinkie Pie. She's my pig."

And that was the start of it. I can't tell you what I looked like when

I heard that, but I'm sure I just stood there like an idiot. Here I was on this island in Florida and this giant pretty girl just told me she had a spirit grandmother and her spirit grandmother lived in her pig. *Great.*

"I'm a Calusa Indian." Sam said this like it was no big deal. Then she started to walk down the street to school. She turned to talk over her shoulder. "Come on, Wolf, your new school awaits."

## How Sam and I Became Friends

I know it's weird that Sam and I became friends and she'd probably say the same thing. Start with the physical differences – she was tall, she had muscles and she was dark, I was short, skinny and pasty white. She spent her whole life working her ass off at a Florida marina, I never had to do anything growing up in a Connecticut suburb. She was really smart and I, well, I knew I could write, but I guess I had to agree with everyone's opinion that I had "behavior issues."

It turned out that Sam didn't have any real friends her own age. That was probably because Sam worked all the time, she dressed in her Calusa outfits at school, and then, most of all, there was the fact that she didn't take shit from anyone.

Me, I was new in town and I lived right across the street, so it made sense that I didn't have any friends except I didn't really have any friends in Connecticut, either. In the beginning, I think Sam was just being nice, she was walking up the road to school, why not take me along?

But I think there were two things that made us friends. First, on that first day out in the street, I didn't say anything when she told me that her pet pig (Pinkie, AKA Nokoomis) saw me watching her from my window. Usually, with my record of saying stuff I shouldn't, I would have said something sarcastic about the pig and her Native American stuff right away, but I was new in town and I thought that might have been how the girls dressed and maybe they all had pet pigs that told them stuff. Who knew?

The second thing that made us friends was that neither one of us liked their family. I remember the first time we ever talked about it was sitting at a picnic table under a palm tree at the marina. That table became our usual meeting spot. On rainy days, Sam didn't have that much to do. It was about a month after I moved to town.

"The first thing you should know is that my mom's a slut."

That got my attention. Kids called each other "slut," but it was something else to say your mom was a slut and sound like you meant it.

"That's kinda strong, isn't it?" It was all I could think to say.

Sam gave me an angry look. "What would you call a woman who has a kid and she doesn't know who the father is?"

"Uh...." I didn't know what to say. I looked at her and tried to figure out if she wanted me to answer. "Yeah." I figured this was a safe response.

So she told me the whole story. Her mom either didn't know who Sam's father was or wouldn't tell her. How Sam found this picture in her mom's drawer under her mom's stash of dope and waited until her mom was drunk to ask about it and found out the guy's name was Bobby Dash and he used to work at the marina but he got caught in a drug bust and then he was an inmate at the state prison. When he got out, he disappeared. Here's a key part: her mom told her when he got caught smuggling drugs, Bobby Dash told everyone he was a Calusa Indian.

I need to tell you something here. Every high school junior in Florida takes a class called "Florida Culture." Since I was brand new in Florida, it was kind of interesting and I paid attention. That's why I know all about the Indian tribes, the trees and the animals in this book. Usually I'm not that smart.

The Calusas were the local Indian tribe in this part of Florida. The Calusas were known as the "shell people" because they mainly ate stuff from the ocean. On islands around here there are big mounds of shells, supposedly left here by the Calusas. The Calusas were really tall and dark-skinned (like Sam and her "father"). The best thing about the Calusas, in my opinion, was they kicked the crap out of the white "settlers" a couple of times, including Ponce de Leon when he was wandering around here looking for the fountain of youth. That always seemed funny to me.

Everybody says the Calusas have been extinct for four hundred years because some other tribe wiped them out. Except Sam told me there's a myth about a secret Calusa settlement down in the Everglades on the Snook River.

After she found the picture in her mom's drawer, Sam went to the library and read everything she could about the Calusas. She had a picture of Bobby Dash, and she showed it to me. I mean, yeah, her "dad" was tall standing next to Sam's mom in the picture, and he definitely had dark hair and dark skin. I didn't argue with her because it was important. She wasn't real proud of the family she had, why shouldn't it be OK to think someone's your dad, even if he isn't around?

So she decided she was a Calusa. She wore shell necklaces and feathers every day. She had that turtle vest. She had all sorts of Indian stuff in her cabin on the boat.

And the animals. She read that when the Calusas die, their spirit lives on in animals, so she got people to give her animals. You never know when a Calusa is going to die, right?

Sam believed—I mean, she *really* believed—that Pinkie Pie was her grandmother.

What did I think of all this? Well, I'd just moved here from Connecticut. She was my only friend. And I liked her. So, at least I didn't say anything stupid.

## Sam and the Turtle Eggs

I was only on the island a month when noises across the street at the marina woke me up one night at around 2 a.m. Something was always going on over there, but this was different; there was a blue light flashing on the wall above my head. Out the window I saw it was a Sheriff's cruiser, parked down by the long dock near Sam's boat. I don't know why I did it, but I got my clothes on and hurried over there.

Sam was just getting into the front passenger seat of the cruiser, and I went around to her side. She rolled the window down.

"What's up?" I looked in at her. Her hair was all messed up, and she had on a t-shirt.

She reached up and pushed the hair out of her eyes. "It's my mom, no big deal, just go back to bed." She started to roll the window up, and I felt the cruiser shift into reverse.

I took a step back, but then I tapped on the window again and it rolled down.

"What, Wolf?" Sam looked frazzled.

"Uh, I'll go with you." I don't know why I said it, I didn't know Sam very well and I didn't know where she was going, but I told you I have this impulsiveness thing and anyway....

"No, go back to bed."

The cruiser began to back out. I tapped on the window again.

It rolled down. "WHAT?" Now I could tell she was pissed. The deputy said something to her. The blue lights and noise from the radio had brought people out of wherever they were sleeping at Granger's out into the yard.

"Really, I want to go." I saw Sam say something to the deputy, and he said something back. I heard the back door click.

"Fine, get in."

There were more blue lights on the beach. When Sam and I got out of the deputy's cruiser, we could see a Sheriff's SUV out on the beach with the headlights shining on a bunch of people sitting in the sand.

Even though I was only there a month, I knew this happened all the time—teenagers hung out at the beach smoking weed and drinking beer. Everybody at school talked about it.

The sheriff's deputy came up next to Sam and pointed. "This way."

As we got close to the SUV, I saw that the people on the sand weren't teenagers. They were adults, and one of them was Sam's mother. I recognized a couple of them, part of the crowd that hung around the marina bait dock all day.

In back of them were a bunch of those little dirt bikes, all on their sides in the dune grass.

A big cop saw Sam and came over to her. "Evening, Sam."

Sam nodded, "Evening, Sheriff."

"Mom's partyin' again."

Sam nodded again. I got the sense this wasn't the first time. At this point, Sam's mom recognized her. "Sam, get your ass home and into bed. Tomorrow's a school day." When she said this, all her friends laughed and shouted.

I had to bite my lip to keep from laughing. Mrs. Granger was flat on her butt in the sand, wearing a bikini top and sweatpants, drunk, and she was yelling at her kid about school. I'm sorry, it was funny. But, luckily, I didn't laugh or say anything, because Sam looked away. I could tell she was embarrassed.

"It's more than usual." The Sheriff said this to Sam, quietly. "They ripped up the turtle nests."

This might not seem like a big deal, but it was. People on the island treated these turtles better than their own children. The sea turtles crawl up on the beach from the ocean, dig holes in the sea grass, and lay their eggs. When the turtle eggs hatch, everybody on the island comes down to watch the babies scurry back to the water. There are fences up around where the turtles lay their eggs and ropes and signs. There are even signs on the road where the turtles cross to get to the other side. All that's pretty hard to miss, even if you are drunk dirt biking.

I walked over there and looked. There were turtle eggs all over the place, and a bunch of them were smashed. Even I felt bad about it, and I don't even care about sea turtles. I walked back to Sam and the Sheriff, and I heard him say something about fines and jail.

"I know you can re-bury the eggs, I read it in a book." It was Sam, and she was talking for the first time since she came to the beach. "If you do it carefully and do it as fast as possible after they've been uncovered."

The Sheriff stood there for a while looking at Sam's mom and her friends. They'd stopped singing "Sweet Home Alabama" and laughing. Now they just looked drunk and sad. Then he made a decision.

"OK, Randy and I will run your mom and the rest of 'em home. You take care of this."

I couldn't believe he was going to do what Sam said. He turned and shouted at everyone, loaded them into the backs of the police cars, and took off.

Sam and I stood there in the dark. I thought I should say something. "Does this happen very often?"

She sighed loudly. "Yeah, I guess so. My mom likes to party. The Sheriff knows she'll go home with me, so they come and get me. A couple times a year, I guess." She sighed again. "But this is the worst. Usually they don't hurt anything." She leaned down and picked up a broken egg. "You should go home. Leave me here."

"No, I'll help, show me what to do."

She looked at me for a couple of seconds. "Really?"

I tried to sound confident. "Sure. I got this. I can sleep anytime."

Sam smiled for the first time that night. "OK, then. I owe you."

Sam and I spent the night on our hands and knees in the dune grass, making new turtle egg mounds. There was a half moon, so we saw what we were doing. An hour after he left, Sheriff Pruitt came back in his own truck in regular clothes with some Cokes and chips. And he stayed there all night, too, putting back up all the fences and signs and helping with the eggs. By the time the sun came up, we were done. Pruitt gave us a ride back home.

We stopped in the marina lot. The Sheriff rubbed his face. "Big night."

Sam: "Yup."
Pruitt: "See you next time."
Sam: "Guess so."

I don't know why I never had a best friend. For a while, I blamed it on the Greggy thing. For a couple of years, kids called me Cujo and shit like that. I tried to laugh about it, but seriously, who wants to be friends with a kid that other kids make fun of? I already had a complex about being adopted, and the Greggy thing just made it worse. Anyway, Sam became my best friend. And I liked that, even with her crazy life and everything.

## Our First Plan and Kissing Sam

After the big meeting at the library with Officer Hultz and Sheriff Pruitt, I walked to school with Sam. She was pretty sad, worried her spirit grandmother was going to disappear if Pinkie wasn't buried right. I tried to tell her we could do something about it, but that didn't work, mainly because between the two of us, she was always the one with a plan and I was always the one who was depressed.

I didn't see Sam the rest of the day. That was unusual, since we usually walked home together.

Saturday, I texted her, but she didn't respond.

I sat in my room that night, not knowing where she was and not hearing from her, and I felt a little sick.

It's hard to understand what it is between Sam and me. I always relied on her when I was scared of stuff. Nothing seems to bother Sam, and lots of stuff bothers me. And now this thing with Pinkie Pie? I mean, I suppose it's hard enough when your pet dies, but when your pet is the spirit of your grandmother? I know I can't figure it out, but I guess if there were a time when Sam would be upset, this would be it.

I waited until it was quiet downstairs in the house. Joel always fell asleep after dinner while he was watching golf on television. When my mom went to bed around ten, she'd shake him awake and he'd stumble to bed with her. I heard those noises from downstairs, the doors closing, the toilets flushing.

It was easy making it downstairs and outside because Joel snored and grunted when he slept and my mom wore these big noise-cancelling headphones to bed. Neither of them could hear anything.

Along with everything else at Granger's, there were people who slept in the shacks and boathouses. I've never figured out who they were, but I can definitely tell you they weren't hanging out with Joel and the other golfers at the Inn.

Sam herself slept in an old broken down sailboat, tied at the furthest end of the dock on the canal. When I first asked her about it, she just laughed, although I could tell she didn't think it was funny.

Her mother lived above the bait shop and I think the reason Sam didn't sleep over there was her mom kept having guys over.

I took a big breath and moved around the edge of the marina, trying to stay out of their big streetlight. It was a foggy night, and there was a rainbow around the light. I could make it to Sam's boat fine in the daylight, but when it was dark it was going to be harder.

Right away, those dogs Tripod and Bailey followed me, and I tried to get them to go away, but then I figured if I made any noise, someone might see a dog and think it was them.

I made it to the edge of the first boathouse and stood still, trying to catch my breath. Down in the canal I could hear mullet splashing on the surface, and there was an owl hooting somewhere. Because of the fog, my ears felt like I had cotton in them. I smelled somebody smoking dope, but that wasn't unusual. Then I got scared and thought about getting out of there and going back to my house. And then I thought about what Sam said when I was scared about something. She'd call me a titty-baby. Titty-baby was one of her favorite expressions. She'd learned it from one of the fishing guides. That made me smile and feel better.

I was farther away from the streetlight now, but I knew I was next to the first shack because the shark cage was right in front of it. People catch sharks on the beach at night, but I never figured out what that shark cage was for.

As quietly as I could, I shuffled through the crackling banyan leaves on the sand and moved to the next shack. I could hear my own breathing, and as I moved under a screen window I heard low talking inside.

I took another big breath and tried to find the third shack. I hit my leg hard on something and it was all I could do not to yell. I reached down and felt around and realized it was a lawnmower on its side.

Carefully, I put my foot on the dock behind the third shack. I didn't want to fall in the canal. The docks were usually slippery with fish guts and moss and shit on them. I just needed to make it down to the end of the dock. I squinted into the darkness and fog, and I tried to visualize the canal. I was probably past the big barge with the crane on it they kept over there. Then, right in front of me, I saw her boat. As quietly as I could, I knocked on the side next to one of the portholes. And then I whispered, "Sam?"

"Who's there?" Her voice was really loud and that scared the shit out of me. I jumped back a little.

"It's me." There was a silence. The fog kind of muffled my voice, but it also made it louder like I was talking with a blanket over my head.

"Wolf?"

"Yeah."

I moved my mouth close to the screen on the porthole.

"Sam?" I stopped and listened.

"Leave me alone."

That stopped me. I didn't think that Sam wouldn't want me to come.

"Why?" I knew it sounded dumb, but I couldn't think of anything else to say.

From the middle of the island, I heard the church bells going off, and I counted to eleven. Then I heard a screen door open back up at the shacks and I felt a weight step onto the dock. I froze and held my breath. I heard someone pissing in the canal. I waited, and the pissing went on a long time. The noise stopped, the steps on the dock went away, and I heard the door slam again.

I leaned back to the porthole and repeated myself. "Why?"

There was a really long silence, and then Sam said in a voice that was way too quiet for her. "I'm sad."

I knew that, but I didn't know what to say.

"Sad, like how?" Just when the words came out, I knew how lame they sounded. I felt like biting my tongue in punishment. *"Sad like how?" Stupid!*

But she answered, "I'm sad about Pinkie and I'm sad about Nokoomis."

I still didn't know what to say.

"Uh, Sam. Can I come in?" It was all I could think of. Plus, I was getting tired bending over and whispering in the porthole. Plus, I thought if we were going to have a serious conversation, we needed to do it face to face.

There was another long silence. Then I heard her moving around and she came back to the porthole. "Yeah, I guess, come on aboard."

Her room—she called it a "cabin"—was like something you'd see in a fairy tale movie. It had a low ceiling and was all dark wood. There was a single bed under a kind of shelf-overhang thing. There was a damp smell like in a tent after a rainstorm, but there was also a new, herb-y smell.

There were books everywhere and Indian stuff, shells, feathers and even something on the wall that looked like a combo spear and shovel, sort of like a spork on a stick. The cabin was lighted by candles, and they were all over the place. I'd been in there lots of times, but now, on the little desk in the corner there was a picture of Pinkie Pie draped with a shell necklace. There was a ring of candles around it like a shrine. Next to it was an incense burner with a flame going on top of a thin stick. I figured that was the new smell.

Sam sat on her bed, and she saw where I was looking. "I've been talking to her."

I stood there uncomfortable, trying to take this in. *She's been down here talking to her dead pig/grandmother?*

"Pinkie needs to be buried by September 15th. That's the next full moon."

I tried to think of something to say, and I couldn't. So I didn't say anything. That was something good I could say about all those counseling hours in the Sped Shed. It was Ms. Gordon's idea that I didn't have to say something to everything. That only got me in trouble. The silence went on, and I tried to visualize a calendar. September 15$^{th}$ was the next Saturday, a week away.

"And that's Heritage Day. How will we do it then with all those people?" I thought about that, and I remembered last year just after we moved here. Everybody in town celebrated the island's "heritage" all weekend. Everyone dressed up as pirates because they think there were pirates here long ago. There was a parade and a big dinner at the Inn on Saturday night. It all seemed kind of lame to me, but it seemed important to the people here. The Governor even comes to the dinner.

How do I know all this? Joel was the chairman of this year's Heritage Day, and I'm sure it was part of his grand plan to suck up to the people at the Inn. It's all I heard him talk about for the past six months.

And then Sam started to cry. "She says she needs to be buried in sacred ground. I can't lose my grandmother's spirit or I'll never find my father." And then the tears really poured down her face.

She stopped for a second. "And it's their stupid pirate day. Pirates didn't find this island, the Calusas did."

I knew that. Just like I heard Joel talk about Heritage Day, I heard Sam talk about how Heritage Day should be about the Calusas, not the pirates. It sincerely pissed her off.

I sat down on the bed next to her, but I really didn't know what to do, so I just sat there quiet, while she sobbed. I wondered about Pinkie telling her that she needed to be buried in sacred ground. And in the middle of Heritage Day weekend. *How, exactly, would that happen?*

Around us, the boat creaked as I felt the rocking from the wake of a boat going up the canal. I put my arm around her shoulder because it seemed like I should. Actually, since she was so much bigger than me, I had to reach up to hold her shoulder. Even when she was leaning over.

Right away, I smelled our smells. As usual, she smelled a little fishy from loading bait at the dock. And my trip across the marina parking lot made me sweat and my armpit—the closest armpit to Sam's face—really stunk. But, I liked the way my arm felt around her shoulders. I hoped she wouldn't say anything about my armpit.

Then, she moved closer to me and put her head on my shoulder. I didn't know what to do about that. I sat there for a minute or two while she cried quietly, and then I kissed the top of her head.

I don't know why I did that. It just seemed the thing to do, maybe something I remembered my mom doing when I was little. I held on to her shoulder and waited. Her crying seemed to slow down. I wondered if she noticed the kiss.

Then Sam lifted her head and kissed me. Just like that. I mean *really* kissed me. Not a little lip brush, but she had her mouth slightly open and she kind of moved her lips around my lips. And then I felt her tongue. I guess I never imagined that Sam Granger would have a tiny, pointed tongue, but she did. I wondered what to do with my tongue and so I let it come forward and touch hers. It was a little weird, but it felt good and it was like warm water had been poured in my bloodstream, starting at my head.

That was my first kiss. Ever.

I had imagined kissing a hundred, maybe a thousand girls, but I never, ever, imagined my first kiss would be with Sam Granger. Sam was my best friend. The kind of friendship you'd have with another guy, if I had any guy friends.

Then I realized I just had my one arm around Sam's shoulder and my other arm was just hanging limp, not doing anything. This left us sitting next to each other kind of sideways kissing.

Our tongues were doing a little dance back and forth. Was I supposed to know what comes next?

Suddenly, Sam pulled away and stood up. For the first time I realized she was just wearing a long t-shirt. I couldn't believe I just had my first kiss with a girl with her only in what she slept in. I think she realized it, too, because she turned and pulled a sweatshirt out of a drawer and pulled it on, even though it was like ninety degrees in there.

She sat down at her little table and looked at me. I was expecting her to call me a pervert or a weirdo. Maybe order me off her boat. But, she didn't say anything and that was weird.

"We should do something about Pinkie Pie." It was the first thing that came to me.

She only nodded and she looked at me for a long time like she was wondering about something.

This quiet Sam was all new. I waited, and she just sat there and looked at me.

I was desperate. She was my best friend and now I had just kissed her. What did I need to do?

Did you know that you can learn to kiss on the Internet? I went home that night, and I Googled "how to kiss," and then I looked it up on YouTube. I know this makes me sound like a loser and this is the kind of stuff I didn't want people to know when I wrote this. Oh, well.

At first, I got a lot of porn. There are lots of porno flicks with the title "How To Kiss." Needless to say, they are about a lot more than that and I was tempted to watch, but I really needed to know how to kiss, not the other stuff.

I thought my kissing with Sam went pretty well, but I needed to make sure. I found a video that was supposed to be a joke where two girls kissed and then explained what felt good and what didn't. I even took notes:

1. Be gentle, but firm. No going after a girl's lips like a dog with a ball. (That's what one of the girls said, I didn't say it.) But don't just let your lips lie there, either. Your lips are an extension of your affection. (Again, I didn't come up with this, I would never write something like this, although it made sense.)
2. No slobbering like a dog. (I think the one girl in the video had a dog)
3. No biting, but one of the girls said "maybe later." I didn't want to think about that. I was having a hard enough time learning to kiss. Biting? I got in trouble for biting once.
4. Use the tongue gently, no tongue down the throat. (Got that one, made sense.)
5. Turn sideways so noses don't hit. (I figured that out when I was kissing Sam, but it's good advice for someone who's never done it before.)
6. Take a break every now and then to breathe. If you need to breathe, your partner does, too.
7. Noises. Little moans are OK, growling (the dog girl again) and loud stuff should be avoided.

That was my list. I was happy that I did most of this stuff with Sam, but I was glad to learn about the tongue part. That was an area I was worried about. Along with the videos and articles on the web, there were all sorts of health warnings about kissing, but I didn't read them. That didn't seem like good stuff to think about.

## We Start Figuring Things Out

The next day, I helped Sam with her chores around the marina. It was a weird day, because she was still quiet. I could tell she was still sad about losing Pinkie. At least I hoped that was it. I didn't want her feeling bad because we kissed.

After lunch on the picnic table, I stood up to go back over to my house and she stood up, too. I stood there awkwardly. Did she want me to kiss her goodbye? I froze. Right there in the marina yard? Instead she spoke. "What should we do?"

This totally confused me. Was she still asking me about Pinkie, or was this about kissing? Quickly, I looked up and down the road.

"Uh…." I stalled for time, as I was trying to think.

"About Pinkie Pie." One side of me was relieved she wasn't talking about kissing. Another side of me was disappointed she wasn't talking about kissing.

I still couldn't figure out what to say, but then I came up with something. "We need to know where the sacred burial grounds are."

She kind of smiled and nodded. "I'll ask Nokoomis." And then, "Meet me on the boat tonight."

As I walked up to my house, I was confused. When I said we needed to find out where the sacred burial grounds were, I thought maybe we'd look it up or maybe find a museum. I didn't know we were going to take orders from a dead frozen pig.

I met her back in her cabin on the sailboat at nine that night and I sat next to her at the table. Just to look official, I grabbed a pad of graph paper I had in my room and brought it along. She didn't say anything and I didn't know what to say, so I just smiled. This was all pretty weird. I didn't know if it was because of Pinkie getting killed or us kissing or what, but all of a sudden, things had changed between us.

She didn't smile back. Instead, she just looked at me with those wide black eyes. She had her feather behind her ear. "I'm losing Nokoomis."

I didn't understand this, but I didn't want to upset her any more by asking a stupid question. So, I decided to say something medium. "Losing?"

All of a sudden, she began to cry. Again. The third time I'd seen Sam Granger cry in three days.

"She's hard to understand. Her voice wasn't clear." She used a Kleenex to blow her nose.

Then she really started to cry. Not just dripping tears, but sobbing with her shoulders going up and down. When she didn't slow down, I got up, moved around the table and sat next to her. I put my arm around her and it felt good. It seemed like the thing to do, but I couldn't help wondering if we were going to kiss again.

Finally, her crying slowed down. "I think she said in sacred ground under the biggest banyan." She said it quietly, but it totally took my mind off the possible kiss.

"Wendell, what should we do?" My mind went blank. First of all, she never called me "Wendell." She always called me "Wolf."

Second, she was still asking me what to do. She was the one who came up with things to do, what time we were going to do them, and all the rest.

All of a sudden, my mouth was dry. Gently, I let my hand fall away from her shoulder, even if it meant I wasn't going to kiss her again. I looked at her and she seemed to be waiting. This was really confusing.

"I, uh…." Then I thought of my graph paper. I pulled it over and picked up a pen. I tried to think of something to say that mainly wouldn't sound dumb and maybe make Sam feel better.

"Let's make a list." I let my voice trail off. This is where Sam usually took over if she hadn't already begun bossing me around. I looked at her and she just nodded. Just to get us started, I wrote—down at the bottom of the page—"bury Pinkie Pie."

As I was writing it, I thought about how stupid the words looked. How would we ever get a frozen pig out of the Animal Shelter and buried? And then I got frustrated with Sam, even though she was sitting there in tears and for the first time I couldn't remember, she couldn't figure out what to do. I mean, I'd always put up with all the Calusa shit, with the feather in the hair and the shell necklaces and the talking to the animals. But I didn't say anything about me being frustrated. Was it because she was my friend or because I hoped she'd kiss me again?

An hour later, we had a bunch of stuff written on the graph paper. That time of year there were big storms, and it started to rain outside. The heavy drops sounded like someone was tossing little rocks on the deck above us. The wind from the storm flickered the candles around the picture of Pinkie Pie.

I reached over and smoothed out the bottom of the page so we could see the whole thing. On the top next to "bury Pinkie Pie," Sam insisted I write "in sacred ground."

And then, the date, Saturday night, September 15. And then, "full moon."

On the other side of the page, I wrote "biggest banyan." As I wrote the words on the page, I had to keep from saying anything. This information came from a grandmother's spirit in a dead pig frozen in the animal shelter and communicated somehow to a girl who thought she was an extinct Indian. OK, then, but I still wrote it down.

Sam spoke up. "If it's sacred ground, it will be a shell mound." She took my pen and wrote "shell mound" on the page. I knew there were shell mounds around here, but I didn't think there were any on Banyan Island.

We talked about the "biggest banyan." Some banyan trees are huge. They are the kind of trees that send out vines from the ends of their limbs that grow down to the ground and become roots for another tree. The big ones are like circus tents. I mean, you could build a small house under one of these trees, they were so big.

We figured out there were three giant banyan trees on the island. Two of them were in rich peoples' yards on Ocean Avenue, the nicest street in town. All the tourists stopped there to have their pictures taken in front of those trees. The other big banyan tree was in the middle of the golf course at the Inn. It was even called the "Big Banyan." Joel talked about it all the time. He hit his ball to the right of the Big Banyan. He hit his ball to the left of the Big Banyan, he hit his ball OVER the Big Banyan. He'd always brag about how he knew how to get around that f—ing tree when "rookies" hit their balls into the Big

Banyan. And, when you hit your ball into the Big Banyan, there was no getting it out with all those roots and vines in there.

So, according to Sam (and Pinkie, AKA Nokoomis), there was a shell mound under one of those trees. Right away, I had another thought: it didn't matter whether the mound was in there or not, there was no way we were going to bury Pinkie under one of those famous trees. But I kept quiet (which was a big deal for me).

We sat for a while looking at our page filled with notes. Then Sam tore off a new page and wrote "September 14." Then she taped the page to the wooden wall of the boat.

"We have to get Pinkie out of the shelter before the morning of September 15$^{th}$. That's the day they are going to burn Pinkie's body in an oven at the Animal Shelter."

"And how do you know that?"

Her eyes got kind of watery. "Nokoomis told me."

I thought about saying that Nokoomis sure was telling her a lot all of a sudden, but Sam put an end to that when she put her hand behind my head and pulled me closer and kissed me. It was a quick kiss, but I felt her tongue and then she pulled away. She seemed happier.

I picked up the pen and under "Pinkie out of shelter, September 14," I wrote "Learn about Animal Shelter."

Just because I couldn't think of anything else to do, I took a screen shot of a Google Earth satellite shot of the Animal Shelter and taped it to the page.

We both sat next to each other, not talking, looking at the animal shelter page with the satellite picture on it. It was raining harder on the deck above our head, and it was getting hotter and stuffier down in Sam's cabin. September in Florida is like the middle of summer everywhere else.

All of a sudden I felt Sam's hand on my knee. It was just there like a sneak attack. I'm sure I jumped a little, but it felt good. I wasn't thinking about the list anymore, all I could think about was the hand and whether it was going to move or stay where it was. I could feel the sweat dripping down my sides under my t-shirt.

Sam broke the silence. "You need to get inside the shelter and look around."

I almost said "Why me?" but I had to admit, her hand on my knee made me not only keep quiet, but say, "OK." Just for a second, I felt bad. Was I going along with Sam because she was kissing me and stuff or because she was my friend and needed help? Then I didn't feel bad anymore. Plus, I told myself, it made sense. I mean, Sam couldn't very well get in the shelter—they knew it was her pig in the freezer, plus she was six feet tall and wore feathers in her hair—pretty obvious.

"OK." I said it again stronger just to be sure. "OK. I'll do it."

## Planning My Mission to the Animal Shelter

Have I mentioned I was in the band? I was. It all started in grade school when I saw the counselor every day after the dog-bite thing. Everybody talked about me being hyper and impulsive because I was a Russian orphan, and the plan was that I should learn to play the piano. If you want my opinion, asking a kid who's hyperactive to play the piano when he's six is kind of stupid, but my mom bought a piano and I had to practice every day. And, I went to lessons once a week with Mr. Charles, an old guy who lived in an apartment above a cheese shop. I hated the piano and I hated Mr. Charles, and when I was ten, you could join the band at school, and I begged my mother to let me play an instrument if I could give up piano. Me practicing the piano at home and taking me to Mr. Charles was as much a pain to her as it was to me, so she let me.

So, I don't know how this happened, but I ended up playing the frigging flute. (Thought: did all that flute playing help my kissing?) I was the only boy in the flute section at Banyan Island High, and even though I'm a senior, I was the worst flute player in the band. At first, I kept playing because my mom said if I quit I would take piano again. After a while, I played because it was something to do and whenever one of my parents ragged me about not having any friends, I reminded them I was in the band. (Where I didn't have any friends.)

All day, I thought about my assignment: how to get into the Animal Shelter for a look around. I sat in band and thought about it while Mr. Paratore, the band director, yelled at the trumpets and made them play something over and over. Mr. Paratore hated the trumpets. The way you sat in band had to do with how good you were. The first chair flute, a prissy little junior named LuAnn Richardson, sat way up front right next to where Mr. Paratore directed the band. That was fine by me because she was the one who got covered by Paratore's spit when he yelled at the trumpets. I was the 6th chair flute (worst in band), so I sat in the middle, next to the worst clarinet player, Missy Buckler. Missy barely acknowledged I existed, which was typical for a Drama Queen, and she was the head Drama Queen.

Missy was a cheerleader, and if you didn't know this, she reminded everybody every Friday when she came to school in her cheerleader outfit because of the football game that night. And, we had band on Fridays, so I sat next to Missy in her sweater with the orange B on it and the cutout of an angry pirate throwing a football. Banyan Island High's nickname was the Pirates (which pissed Sam off, although she would have been even more pissed off if they were called the Calusas), and there was an idiot kid who dressed up in a pirate costume at the game and marched up and down the sideline.

So I sat there and secretly checked out Missy's legs in her short skirt while Mr. Paratore yelled at the trumpets and I looked down at the floor between us at the huge bag Missy always carried. There was a laminated tag hanging from the strap that read "Banyan Island Animal Shelter Volunteer." And then I remembered. Banyan Island High had a stupid community service requirement. The cheerleaders volunteered at the shelter. Every spring they sold lame stuffed animals as a fundraiser. All of a sudden, I had an idea.

As I put my flute in its case, I said, as casually as I could, "So, Missy, you volunteer at the shelter?"

She looked at me, annoyed. I never talked to her so she didn't have any reason to be annoyed, but that was a DQ trademark: an annoyed look. They practiced in front of the mirror, imagining they smelled something bad. Same look as annoyed.

I pointed down to the tag on her bag. She looked down and back at me. "Uh, yeah." She strung the word "ye—ah" out and raised it at the end like it was a question. All her last words went up at the end. Missy was the ultimate Valley Girl.

Then she looked around, and I was pretty sure she was checking to see if any of her friends saw her talking to me.

"Can anybody volunteer?" It was all I could think of to say.

She stopped and looked me up and down. "Uh, like you think?"

I hated the DQs.

## My Mission to Scout the Banyans

After school, I cruised around town on my bike. It was easy to look at the two big banyans on Ocean Street—all the tourists do—but it wasn't easy to find a way to get underneath them. I used the "lost dog trick."

I started by shouting "Here Fluffy," using a really concerned and whiney voice. Then I just started in under each tree, saying "Here Fluffy," once in a while. The rich people's banyans were all cleared out underneath by their yard workers, so it was easy to see the ground under both of them. Anyway, there was no way there was a shell mound under either of them. There were just roots. They were everywhere. There wasn't really any dirt, not to mention shells.

That left one possibility.

Joel and I didn't talk, and that's not a teenage exaggeration. I mean, we literally didn't talk, unless my mom asked one of us a question that was supposed to be answered by the other. It seemed awkward, but it was just one of the awkward things about our little family. I think by the time I was ten, Joel was done with me. First, there was the whole adoption thing. People say it's not true, but I swear it's harder for a parent to love an adopted kid than their own.

Then there was the thing with Echo and Greggy. Joel wasn't happy about that at all. My mother took me to all the counseling. Joel didn't want to have anything to do with it. All the school conferences on my "learning disabilities," my mom would show up, not Joel. He was pretty much done with me. I was around twelve when I started to call him "Joel" instead of "Dad." I was probably trying to give him a message. I don't think he ever got it. He never told me to stop and I guess that hurt my feelings.

It was a crazy idea. I needed to go golfing with Joel. I had this idea on my own, with no help from Sam. That meant no tears, no kissing, no taking orders from a spirit inside a dead pig. It was all my idea. I was kind of proud of myself. I needed to see if there was a shell mound under the Big Banyan on the golf course.

Joel lived to play golf. And he loved the Big Banyan Inn Club, despite the fact there was some question he could join when we first moved here (maybe because he was Jewish, maybe because he was an asshat, it could have been either). Anyway, he bought one of their condos, got in, started selling the other condos, and to him the club was more important than anything, including me. So, this wasn't going to be easy. The club was his sanctuary and golf was his...anyway, you get the point.

My plan was to talk to Joel when he first got home, but before he had his first drink. He always drank at the club after he played golf, and he was in a good mood when he got home. That was my scientific analysis of when he'd be the easiest to con.

His Cadillac Escalade rolled in the driveway and right after that, I heard him on the stairs. From there, he'd take a direct route across the kitchen, on his way to the "alcove." That's what he and my mom called it. I think it was supposed to be a pantry, but Joel had it set up as a bar. He even had a little sink and icemaker in there. There were rows of liquor bottles on the shelves.

Me being anywhere wouldn't slow him down, he didn't talk to me, especially when he was on his way to a drink. So I stood, as un-awkwardly as I could, blocking the door into the alcove. He came in through the kitchen, stopped, and looked at me. I didn't move. "How's it goin', Wendell?" I swear those were the first words he'd said to me in a month.

"Dad, I need a favor." The words came fast. I needed to spit them out without laughing. Joel looked at me weirdly. Maybe it was because I called him "Dad" and not "Joel."

"What?" He sounded suspicious.

"Umm, a couple of my friends at school were talking about the golf team, and I was thinking of playing on it next spring." I watched his reaction as he tilted his head. There were several unbelievable things in what I'd just said:

1. That I had friends,
2. That I was interested in joining a team,
3. That I, his uncoordinated and totally un-athletic son

(Russian adoptee, not his genes, not his fault), would even think of playing golf.

"Anyway, I wonder if you could teach me?"

He stalled for time. "Um, yeah." He tried to edge past me to get into the alcove to get his drink. I couldn't let him, so I moved slightly to be in his way. He stopped. I'm sure he wanted to tell me to get out of his way, but he didn't want to look like he was jonesing for a drink.

"I was thinking we could start tomorrow after school."

That gave him an out. "I don't golf in the afternoons, too hot."

I was ready for this. "I know it's hot, but I have a big test in the morning and I can't miss school. I might make the honor roll. Could you make an exception just this once?"

I planned it just right. It had to please Joel that I wanted to play the sport he played every day, 365 days a year, and told him how important it was for me to be in school. (I'm sure he didn't believe the crap about the honor roll, but it must have made him wonder.)

I'll not even mention that he might be pleased that his only child, adopted or not, wanted to spend time with him, because I'm sure that didn't occur to him.

And then the most important argument: I was still blocking his sanctuary, the liquor alcove. He'd been home a whole ten minutes and still hadn't had his martini.

I hadn't planned on this part, but my mother walked in the kitchen. She heard part of it and came through for me. "Joel, I think it's nice that Wendell wants to go golfing with you. It seems it's the least you could do to wait to play with him."

My father knew he was beaten. He stepped toward me and, faking affectionate fatherhood, he put his hand on my shoulder. But, instead of a nice pat, he gave me a hard squeeze and a shove as he edged past me to get his drink. "I'll see you at the club at two tomorrow afternoon. Wear a shirt with a collar instead of those stupid t-shirts. And clean shorts. We'll rent you shoes at the pro shop."

OK. That was good.

## My First Mission to the Animal Shelter

The next morning, I skipped school and rode my bike to the Animal Shelter. There was a table in the lobby with a volunteer sign-in clipboard and a bowl of clip-on badges. There was an empty chair behind it, and I guessed the person sitting there had to go to the bathroom or something. I walked up, grabbed a badge, and signed in. Just to be safe, I wrote "H. Potter." Not very original, but it was all I could think of.

I shouldn't have been nervous about getting into the shelter. Everyone was running all over the place, families walking around trying to decide what dog to adopt and old lady volunteers with special red vests.

You could hear the place before you even came in, a bunch of dogs barking and howling. And it smelled, too, a combination of dog shit and cleaning stuff.

I started down the hall toward the barking dogs. On the way, I grabbed a mop leaning against the wall so I'd look official.

The lines of dog cages made me kind of sad. Each cage had one or two dogs in it, and they barked when people came by because they wanted to be adopted and get out of there. The cages were pretty clean, but still, if you were a dog, you wouldn't want to be there. I didn't think their chances were very good. Most of the dogs weren't the kinds people on the island wanted.

"Hey Mop Midget, get down here." I looked around, hoping the guy wasn't yelling at me and then, knowing he was, pissed at being called a midget. Quickly, I looked around to see if anyone heard. "Mop Midget" was a nickname I didn't want. "Get down here." He yelled it again.

I looked around. I was supposed to be on a secret recon mission. The last thing I wanted to do was call attention to "H. Potter" with his unofficial badge. So I headed down the aisle of cages with all the dogs barking at me.

There was a guy down at the end, and he had a mop, too, only he had one of those buckets on wheels that custodians push around schools. The guy was in his twenties with long hair, and he needed a shave.

"Take care of this." He pointed to a pool of dog piss coming out of a cage where there were two dogs. Right away I started to tell him to futz off, but I caught myself. I remember thinking that I needed to tell Ms. Gordon I was getting better at impulse control. Plus, I was on a mission, so I shut up, stuck my mop in the yellow pool, and swished it around.

When I got it all sopped up, I looked over at the guy. He was taking care of a mess on the other side of the "cellblock." He was really skinny, and he had a tight belt holding his jeans up. He saw me looking and pointed to his bucket. "Wring it out in there."

There was this metal thing on the bucket with a handle, but I didn't know what to do. The guy made a loud sighing noise, grabbed my mop from me, stuck it in there, pushed the handle back and forth, and handed it back to me. The mop was all wrung out and sort of clean from the soapy water in the bucket. I thought it was a pretty cool machine.

"Follow me, Mop Midget." The guy took off back down the aisle dragging the bucket on wheels. I followed because I didn't know what else to do.

A couple of hours later, we were done and I was so tired I could barely lift the mop. We cleaned up messes in all five of the aisles, usually piss but sometimes worse. All along, the guy didn't talk much, but as we worked, he got a little friendlier. Along the way, he talked to all the dogs, calling them by name and petting the ones that didn't bite.

He took both our mops and stuck them in a huge sink in a kind of storeroom in the back. Then he opened a little refrigerator and pulled out two Red Bulls and handed me one.

"My name's David, but my friends call me T. Rex." He looked at me. "What's yours, 'H. Potter'?"

I smiled, "Uh, Wendell."

"What's with the "H. Potter" alias?" T. Rex smiled as he asked the question, but I could tell he was suspicious.

I thought fast. *Why the hell didn't I use my real name?* "Uh, my mom thinks I'm at the library."

He gave me a weird look. "Yeah. You with the cheerleaders?"

It took me a second or two, and then I understood what he was asking. *The DQ volunteers.* "No, I go to the high school, but I'm not with them."

"I could tell. You actually did some real work. Them cheerleaders is as useless as a fart in a wind tunnel."

I could tell I had passed his test. I laughed, but then I stopped because I was trying to figure out why a fart would be in a wind tunnel. It didn't make sense, but it was funny.

"This your first time here?"

I nodded. "Yeah."

"Comin' back?"

I thought about how to answer. I didn't come there to volunteer, I was there to look around. But it was kind of fun hanging around with T. Rex, mopping up the floors and talking to the dogs. "Yeah. I think I will." I wasn't lying.

"Want the big tour?" T. Rex smiled at me. My mother would tell him he needed to brush his teeth more.

"Sure."

Almost an hour later, we were done. T. Rex gave me a window squeegee to carry while he carried a spray bottle. That way we'd look like we were working. In addition to the four rows of dogs, there was a big room filled with cats in cages and then a smaller room filled with iguanas in aquariums. As we stood and looked, I asked, as casually as I could, "What happens if the animals aren't adopted?"

T. Rex grunted and motioned with his arm. "This way."

I knew what it was right away. A gigantic oven. I mean, just like when James Bond got trapped in a casket and got shoved in an oven in *Diamonds Are Forever*. I loved that movie. The oven was huge and it had big dials on the outside.

I acted like I didn't know. "What's this?"

"This is what happens when they aren't adopted. You've heard of those "no-kill" shelters? Well, this is a *Hultz* kills shelter. After three weeks here, it's the long march down the hall to the animal kingdom in the sky."

"Just three weeks?"

He shrugged.

I wanted to change the subject, mostly because it made me sad. "And Officer Hultz is in charge of this place?"

T. Rex jerked his head a little. "*Officer* Hultz?" He said "Officer" like he didn't believe it. "Yep, if you call what she does 'in charge'."

I played along. "She doesn't do much work?"

"Yeah, if riding around with your fat ass stuffed in a cart shooting at iguanas is work."

It was getting near noon and I needed to get some more info. "What does she do with the iguanas she shoots?"

He laughed. "There ain't very many. She's a shitty shot."

I laughed to show I appreciated the joke. "Yeah, but the ones she does?"

He gave me a look, and I knew I was asking too many questions. But, this was key stuff.

He gestured across the room at a big metal door. "They go in the freezer until it's time for them to be baked." He gestured at the oven and raised his eyebrows.

I pointed to the freezer. "Is that where they put the pig that was killed this week?"

T. Rex got a sour expression on his face. "That was me. Used a fork lift to get it in my truck, but getting it out of the truck when I got it back here and then into the freezer was a bitch." I acted fascinated, which, actually, I was.

"Can I look?"

T. Rex smiled, like he thought this was a normal question, that a high school kid would want to look at all the dead, frozen animals. Without a word, he stepped over and opened the big freezer door.

It was about the size of our kitchen, and our kitchen is pretty big. And it was cold, seriously cold. There were shelves on the walls, narrow ones on the top and a big wide one around the bottom. On the top shelves, there were maybe ten frozen iguanas, all wrinkled up, all in a row.

On the bottom shelf, there was a huge mound, covered by a bunch of black plastic garbage bags, all taped together. I knew it was Pinkie and I wanted to take a look, but I didn't want to seem obvious.

"When's the next time you're going to fire up the oven?" This is what I needed. I needed to know if Sam was really getting information from her spirit grandmother.

"You really are a Nosy Nellie, aren't you, H. Potter? You're not from one of those animal rights groups are you?" He started to back away, getting ready to leave the freezer.

"No!" I almost shouted it. I tried to figure out something to say, and I remembered him calling all the dogs by their names. He liked the dogs.

We stepped out of the freezer. "I, uh, feel bad for the dogs. I, uh, know some kids who might like to adopt a…big dog…I might adopt one myself, but I need to talk to my parents. I just want to know how much time I have before the next crema-...." I trailed off and waited for him to respond.

He stepped over to the oven and took a clipboard off a hook. "September 15." It was the same date as Nokoomis gave Sam. Nokoomis was right. I think I was a little disappointed. I still wasn't happy being led around by a dead pig.

"It's going to be a big day around here. Hultz can't wait to roast that pig. She's real proud of killing her. She's even calling it her Pinkie Pie Pork Roast."

I rode home in a hurry because I had to meet Joel at the golf course. *Pinkie Pie Pork Roast? Even I was grossed out about that. I didn't think I'd tell Sam. She'd find Hultz and it would be a Hultz Roast instead.*

## Golfing With Joel

Joel wanted to start with some practice on the driving range. I think that's because the driving range is way over by the employee parking lot where people can't see it. Joel didn't want his buddies to see his uncoordinated son until he at least he had a chance to teach me how to hit the ball.

Actually, Joel's embarrassment started in the locker room. "Are you going to wear those?"

I looked at Joel, and then I looked down at what I was wearing. "Those" could apply to several things I wore. My socks were "those," my shoes (with little rubber spikes, which he just gave me) were "those," my shorts were "those," even my underwear were "those" (although I don't understand why underwear is plural—a "pair" of underwear).

So I said "What?" Because I really didn't know.

Joel pointed down. "Those shorts."

I looked down. They were my cargo shorts. The ones with pockets on the sides.

I looked around to see if we were going to have this conversation in front of anyone. The locker room at the Inn was really nice, they have carpet on the floors and nice benches. In the bathroom, they even gave out free razors. There wasn't anyone else there, and it was really quiet.

Even so, I kept me voice down because I knew this was going to be embarrassing. In Joel's opinion, his son—who really wasn't his son—very rarely did things right.

"Yeah."

He stood there looking. I mean, they were cargo shorts. It's not like they were a Speedo. I wore those shorts to school every day.

Joel's shorts were made of this shiny material, they had pleats in the front, and they hung down to his flabby knees. There was a shark or something sewn on the back, above his butt. In my humble opinion (which I didn't express because I needed to get him to take me out on the golf course so I could scout the Big Banyan), my cargo shorts looked better than his shark shorts.

"You don't have any others?"

I really, really wanted to say something. Of course I didn't bring any other shorts. *Sweet Jesus* (Sam's second favorite expression). But I just nodded.

"Just these."

He sighed. "OK, let's go.

It didn't get any better with Joel when I started to practice. I was having fun, but that ended fast. Joel handed me this golf club called a driver with a huge thing on the end you're supposed to hit the ball with. The driver was a Big Betty or something. I swung it around a few times until Joel stopped me. Do you know there's a special grip golfers use where they wind their fingers together around the handle of the club? Well, there is.

Joel grabbed my hands and twisted my fingers to show me.

"Why can't I just hold it like this?" I showed Joel how I wanted to hold it, like a baseball bat, or a stick or a sword, you know, with your hands grabbing it, next to each other.

Joel looked around. There were a couple of guys close to us, hitting their golf balls. I was sure that made Joel nervous.

His voice was low and I could tell he was mad because he gritted his teeth. "Just do it this way, OK, for God's sake. It's the way golfers do it, and you're here to learn to golf. Why is everything so hard with you?"

Well, it was hard. Try wrapping the fingers on one hand around the fingers of the other and holding something. It's not easy. But I needed to remember why I was there.

They use these special yellow balls on the driving range, and I balanced one on the little tee Joel gave me. It fell off twice before I got it to stay.

Joel told me where to put my feet and how to stand.

I did the special golf-grip. I missed the ball on my first try. Totally. I laughed.

Joel blew breath out his mouth so I could hear him, and he looked behind him to see if the guys were watching. They weren't. "It's not funny," he said.

Now I was a little nervous. I wasn't nervous before, but I caught Joel's nervousness from him. I didn't know this was going to be such a big deal. I mean, I didn't want to look stupid out there, either.

So I concentrated.

The next one, I skimmed the ball and it shot off to the right, toward the other guys. *Not bad*, I thought, at least I made contact. "All right," I said, loud enough for everybody to hear. Maybe this was going to be fun, after all.

"Sorry!" Joel yelled it to the other guys. "Teaching the kid to hit a few."

I don't know why, but that really pissed me off. Maybe it was "the kid." I don't think Joel ever called me his "son."

So I focused, but it wasn't fun anymore. I hit the next ball sort of straight, not very far, but it was at least in front of us. He didn't say anything, but he grabbed his bag and headed for our golf cart. "Let's go."

So I grabbed my bag (it was heavy) and I followed. This wasn't going to be a father/son bonding day, it was a mission.

The Big Banyan was in the middle of the fifth hole. I did OK on the first four holes. I just watched Joel and tried not to hit the ball as hard as he did. I even told him I wanted to carry my own bag and not ride in his cart, because that's the way they did it on the golf team. I needed to get him comfortable with me being out there so I could look around the tree.

On the fifth hole, Joel went first and he hit his ball way over the Big Banyan and then he took off in the cart.

Carefully, I hit the ball as straight as I could, right at the tree. It rolled part of the way, but it almost made it. By this time, Joel was out of sight, way down the fairway. I looked around and couldn't see anyone, so I picked up my ball and threw it into the vines and limbs. Just to be safe, I shouted, "Whoa, hit my ball into the tree." I ducked under the Big Banyan and followed my ball in.

I had to wait for my eyes to adjust, it was that dark in there. The limbs and vines coming down from above and then going into the ground made it like a cave with stalactites (or stalagmites, never could remember which was which from Science class (Sorry, Mr. Zeiter)).

There were lizards everywhere, scurrying up and down. Lizards really didn't bother me, but when there were so many of them, I started to worry about what else might be in there. The ground was covered by dead banyan leaves the size of dinner plates. I didn't know what else to do, so I started pushing leaves around with my Big Betty, seeing if I could tell if there were shells under there. I made my way around the tree, weaving in and out of the limbs coming down and into the ground. Every couple of steps I could see better when a shaft of light would shine through the leaves overhead. All of a sudden I felt something gooey on my face and, without thinking, reached up to wipe it away. I guess it was a wet spider web because when my hand got to my forehead it collided with something big that I squished right against my head. I don't know if you've ever seen the spiders in Florida, but they're huge and hairy—much bigger and hairier than the spiders in Connecticut. When I squished it, it made a crunching sound, and because it was on my head, it was really loud. Anyway, I needed to get it off my head and face, so I was using both hands to wipe it off when the little spikes on my golf shoes caught on a root and I fell down.

When you fall in a bunch of banyan leaves, it makes a huge crash, almost like you dropped a bunch of pans on the floor in the kitchen. I rolled around to try to get the spider web off and I ended up feeling like I had a spider web all over my body, not to mention the gooey spider shit squashed on my forehead. And then my legs began to sting and I knew I had landed in fire ants. Fire ants' stings are a bitch.

Right then I heard, "Wendell." It was Joel, but he sounded pretty far away, so between the spider attack and the fire ants, I just kept rolling around in the banyan leaves.

All of a sudden, as I was thrashing around in the leaves, I realized I was on a hill. It was hard to tell because it was under the leaves and the banyan limbs and vines came down to the ground all around me, but my head was a lot higher than my feet. I got up on my hands and knees, and I rolled downward. It was definitely a hill. I felt around with my hands. Shells. *All Right!*

"Wendell?" It was Joel again, and he was closer. I was quiet and poked my head up to see where he was. He sounded pretty close, although it was hard to tell from the middle of the banyan.

"Wendell?" I scrunched down. He was right outside the tree. I lowered my voice so it would seem further away. "Yeah, just a sec, I hit my ball in here."

"Goddamit. Just take a penalty and hit a new ball. We've already been out here all day." My dad, Joel. A prime asshat. But I'd found the Calusa shell mound. I couldn't wait to tell Sam.

## We Plan Some More

Sam treated me like I was a big hero. It was just after ten that night, and I sat with her at her little table. In front of me, Sam placed a Yoo-hoo and five of those tiny bags of Fritos. I knew she stole them from the bait shop, but still, they were my favorites, and I was glad she got them. She even got me some cream for my ant bites.

It was hotter than usual down in Sam's cabin. Instead of her overalls she was wearing her old gym shorts. I knew she wore these shorts when it was hot, but I'd never really paid attention to them. Now they looked good, even though they still had paint and grease stains on them. She was next to me on the bench, our now-usual seating arrangement.

Sam was quiet as I told her about what I'd seen at the shelter, and she just nodded when I told her she (and Nokoomis) were right that September 15 was the day Hultz was going to cremate Pinkie (I didn't tell her about Hultz calling it a Pinkie Pie Pork Roast).

I told her about golfing with Joel, and she nodded and smiled. She was impressed that I had decided on my own to check out the Big Banyan, but she wasn't surprised there was a shell mound in there. She knew this would happen. Nokoomis had predicted it. *Right.*

I taped the scorecard from the golf course up on the graph paper. It had a map on the back. On the map, I circled where the Big Banyan was. We both studied it without saying anything.

Instead of looking at what I'd written, Sam said, "Do you think Missy's hot?"

Immediately I began to answer like Sam was still my best friend. We always talked about this kind of stuff.

"She's...." And then I stopped. Sam had her legs folded up in front of her with her arms around them. I tried not to look too closely, but I could see she'd shaved her legs up to her knees. She'd never done that before. Her legs were hairier than mine. Then I saw there were soft black hairs on the backs of her thighs leading up to her shorts. I had to stop talking. I didn't want to tell Sam I thought Missy was hot, and all

I could think about was Sam's thighs.

All of a sudden, I felt extra warm, and I could feel my face get red. Because I couldn't think of anything else to do, I pushed myself off the bench and said, "I've got to take a piss." That's the way Sam and I talked, but now it seemed wrong to say that to her. Everything was changing.

I went up to the deck. There wasn't a bathroom on her boat, so Sam always used the porta-pottie on the dock because she's a girl. But, I'd been pissing off that deck for a year, ever since I met Sam.

But then I stood on the deck and couldn't go. I needed to go, but I was frozen because Sam could hear me and we'd been kissing. Anyway I stood there with my…anyway, I just stood there.

From down below I heard Sam call, "What's going on up there?"

I scrambled off the boat, off the dock, and onto the shore next to the mangroves. There, I could go. Then I hurried back.

"Thought I heard something," I said as I sat back down. I knew that didn't make any sense. Of course I heard something, there were all kinds of noises out there, music playing, bushes rustling, water splashing.

"OK, where were we?" I tried to sound business-like.

"I asked you if you thought Missy was hot." Of course Sam remembered what she was saying. When Sam wanted to know something, she was like Tripod with a bone.

"Well, she sure as shit thinks she is." I said it to get her to think about something else.

Sam laughed, but then she looked at me closely. I tapped the plan and changed the subject. "We need to get Pinkie out of the shelter before the morning of the 15th. But we need to bury her the night of the 15th. The Big Banyan is in the middle of everything. There's a road right next to the golf course, a bridge over the bayou where people can look down on the golf course, and the Sheriff keeps his boat on the bayou about a hundred yards away. I know you say we're getting Pinkie out, but Pinkie is a 350-pound frozen pig. I don't know how we'd get Pinkie out of there and buried in a mound covered with roots."

"Don't talk like that, Wendell. Of course we'll get her out. Nokoomis says we will, and she is depending on us." I know I looked skeptical. I don't know if that was the reason, but Sam took my hand.

Having her hand on mine was like getting a low-level shock. I tried to concentrate.

She just sat there looking calm.

"Without getting caught." I finished.

We both just sat and looked at those dates on the plan. I don't know what Sam was thinking, but to me it looked hopeless. Everything looked hopeless; getting Pinkie out, burying her, all of it. I just kind of held my breath. I wanted it to work for Sam because she was my best friend, but I wanted it to work even more because we were kissing. I was hit by a new thought. Was Sam my girlfriend? And then I had another thought, can your girlfriend still be your best friend?

And then, I don't know why I said it, but I spoke up. "We can figure it out. I'm sure we can make it happen."

She looked at me like I'd said the most important thing in the world. "Oh, Wendell." And then she kissed me again. I felt really good, but afterwards I wondered if the reason I said we could make it happen was that I was competing with a dead spirit pig.

Then I realized I lived in a new universe. Life had changed for me. There was the pre-kiss universe where I would maybe do stuff for Sam because she was my best friend. Now I lived in the post-kiss universe.

So I said it again. "I'm sure we can do it."

Then she kissed me with her hand on the back of my neck. It was our best kiss yet.

# Reggie

It was dark, and I felt the vibration on my phone on the table next to my bed. I picked it up and squinted: 5:30 a.m. It was a message from Sam:

**"Meet me at the picnic table. Now."**

At first, I was confused. Then I was pissed. *5:30 in the morning?* Then, I have to be honest, I thought about the kissing the night before. I got up and headed to Sam's.

Sam scared the crap out of me when she stepped out of the darkness by the picnic table. She kissed me on the cheek, and she smelled like coffee. "Follow me. We're going down here." She gestured down the dock beyond her boat and took my hand.

I didn't move. I didn't understand what she was doing. But, she had my hand. At first, I just squinted, it was dark and I couldn't see, anyway, but all I could remember down there was a wall of bushes at the end of the dock. I always thought her boat was the last one in line. I couldn't imagine where she wanted to go, but I followed.

After a couple of steps, she dropped my hand, clicked on the light on her phone and pushed some of the bushes aside. I could see the dock kept going. "This way," she said, as she stepped past the branches she was holding.

On the other side, I could see a shape of a boat tied up to the dock. There was a dim light coming from the back of it. As we got closer, I saw it was an old flats boat, the kind of boat some of the fishing guides used to go way up in the shallow water near the shore to fish.

When we got close, I saw the light was coming from a little tent in the back. It looked like a lean-to you see them build on survival shows. There was a big tarp hung over the center console where the steering wheel was. The tarp was tied down to the sides of the boat. I thought I could smell dope, but maybe it was just because this was where I thought dope would be smoked for sure.

"OK, I got him," Sam whispered. I heard a scraping noise, and a shape came out of the lean-to and was backlit by the light. I could tell it was a guy. Also, that he was skinny. He was wearing some kind of basketball jersey, and there was sweat on his shoulders.

He grinned at me, held his hand out for a slap, and said, "You be Wendell Wolf. I seen you around. Come aboard, Mon." I know it sounds like a cliché, a Jamaican guy in dreadlocks saying "Mon," but that's what he said. He wore a red knit hat—they call them 'Rastacaps' in Florida—over his hair. He had two gold teeth in front.

I knew him. His name was Reggie, and he did lawn work at the Inn. You'd always see him riding around town in an old golf cart with palm fronds piled up in back. I also knew he was Sam's friend, and since I was Sam's only other friend, I was jealous of him and avoided him. I know, I'm weird.

He was also a fishing guide. From my bedroom window I saw him picking up people at the Granger's dock in his flats boat. The rumor around town was that he used that boat for picking up dope, too.

I looked at Sam and whispered, "What's going on?"

She just shrugged.

"Come inside." The guy had the lowest voice I'd ever heard. He was like a back-up singer on one of my mom's soul CDs. Reggie motioned to us, and then he ducked back under his shelter. Sam had to really bend over to get under the tarp because she was tall, but it was easier for me. Reggie pointed to two low beach chairs. "Take a load off. Get some coffee."

I sat down and looked around. There was a kerosene lantern hanging from a metal bar over the steering wheel, and it was turned down low. Reggie turned back from a little gas stove and handed me a cup. I wanted to say I didn't drink coffee, but I just shut up. I noticed Sam held a cup of coffee, and Reggie picked one up next to where he sat down. That was probably the coffee smell on Sam's breath. *She was here before she texted me. Shit.*

Sam started in. "Nokoomis told me we need Reggie's help."

"I can't believe this...." I started to talk, but then I stopped. I felt my face get hot and my eyes got a little unfocused like they do when I'm really pissed. I even felt a little headache. Reggie and Sam both looked at me. I just shook my head, embarrassed. I was so jealous all of a sudden. I'd been the only one helping Sam. Just me, Wendell Wolf, loser Russian adoptee. I'd been the one putting up with all the Nokoomis-is-my-spirit-animal bullshit. And I'd been the one she'd been kissing. After I took a breath or two, I thought the kissing might be the reason I was jealous.

"Wendell." I could tell Sam knew what I was thinking. "It's Wednesday morning. We only have three days. You said so yourself. Nokoomis thought Reggie could help." She reached over to my chair and took my hand. Right in front of Reggie. I was embarrassed at first and thought about pulling my hand away, but then I changed my mind and held her hand harder. I wanted Reggie to see.

And then I thought about what she'd just said. I didn't know why we needed Reggie, but I didn't want to look stupid, so I kept quiet. Plus, up to then, we'd been taking orders from Nokoomis, why should this be any different? So, I just nodded.

"You kids want another coffee?" Reggie held up his cup.

Both of us shook our heads, but just for something to do, I took a sip of the coffee he gave me earlier. It was great. Coffee mixed with milk and a lot of sugar. I really liked it, and I took a bigger sip.

"How you plan to get d' big pig outta d' shelter?" Reggie looked at Sam, and then at me. Reggie pronounced "the" as "d." He had a singsong Jamaican accent.

Then I was pissed that Sam shared our secret, but I stopped thinking about that when Sam looked at me and said, "That's up to Wendell."

"Me?" I said it before I thought about it. Then Reggie smiled, and I saw all his gold teeth. "D' pig, Mon. You kids need to move Pinkie, d' big pig, right?"

I nodded, but I still didn't understand what we were doing. *Why was I in charge?*

"Pinkie, he's a 350-lb pig, right?" I nodded. Reggie pronounced "350" as "tree hundert, fitty." Reggie kept talking. "My girl Sammy here tell me how you make it into d' shelter and onto d' golf course. Smart work, Mon."

At first I was unhappy he called Sam "my girl" and "Sammy," but then I focused on what he'd just said. *"Smart work, Mon."*

I tried to put it together. *Reggie thought I did smart work?* I was happy an adult like Reggie thought I did a good job at something.

"How you get d' big pig outta d' shelter?" Reggie repeated his question. It brought me back to reality.

I kind of shook myself and focused on Pinkie and the shelter. "Uh, well, the shelter has this back door, right, and it's right next to the big freezer where Pinkie Pie is." I paused, hoping this would be enough.

Reggie took a big sip of coffee. "And?"

I looked at Sam for help.

She just looked back at me with her beautiful eyes, and then she took my hand.

"I, uh." My mind was totally empty. I didn't have one fringing idea how we were going to get frozen Pinkie out of there. And then I thought of that guy at the shelter, T. Rex. "Uh, there's this guy...." I looked up, and both Sam and Reggie were watching me, listening. I thought I felt Sam's hand tighten on mine. "And, uh, T. Rex is a pretty good guy...."

Both Sam and Reggie nodded.

That gave me a little confidence. "And, uh, I think I can get him to let me in."

Reggie nodded and interrupted. "How you gonna get dat big pig outta dere?"

My mind went blank again. I was good at making lists, but this *doing* stuff was hard. I looked over at Sam, because she was the one who was always in charge of doing stuff. She just nodded like I was supposed to go on. Then I thought about Reggie's question.

I tried to think. "Uh, T. Rex and I are working on that."

"Need to be before Saturday morning, right? Dat's when Hultz do d' oven?"

I just nodded. Sam had told Reggie everything.

"So you gonna take her out Friday night." It was a statement, not a question from Reggie.

I nodded again.

Reggie got up and rummaged around in the compartment behind the cooler. He sat back down and unfolded a big piece of paper. Then he reached under the tarp and his hand came back holding a bucket that he turned upside-down between the three of us. He spread the paper out on the bucket. It was the kind of map that sailors use—a chart, I thought they called it—with all sorts of numbers and squiggly lines all over it. Then he reached up, got the hanging lantern and handed it to me. "Gimme light here." He found a pen in his shirt pocket and used it to point. "You get d' pig outta d' shelter, and deliver her here at eleven p.m. Friday night."

I squinted at where he pointed. "Where?"

He tapped his pen kind of hard on the map like he was impatient. I couldn't help it if I couldn't figure out a stupid boat map. "Here d' bridge." I saw that, the line going from the island to the mainland. There were all sorts of markings in the water around it. I knew that's where the tall boats waited for the drawbridge to open.

"D' boat landing. Down at d' far end, Mon, away from d' lights."

I saw where he pointed. It was the public boat landing on the mainland before you got to the bridge. It was where everyone put their boat in the water and then left their trailers in a big parking lot. There were a couple of places in the lot that sold bait and a booth out front on the road where you paid to use the ramps.

Sam sat back and pushed her hair off her sweaty forehead. I'd never noticed her do that before. She spoke: "So we have a plan on where to take Pinkie after we get him out of the shelter." She looked up, and Reggie and I nodded. "And Wendell is working with his guy to get him out." Sam gave my hand a little squeeze. I don't know if that's why, but I heard myself say one word. "Right."

Afterwards, Sam and I stood in the dirt lot in the marina just as the sun was making an orange glow coming up out of the bay. There were noises all around, but they seemed normal—the wind, dogs barking in the distance, some bird squawking in a tree. Sam stood a little closer than usual, then she put her arms around me. It was a little awkward because at first she pinned my arms to my sides. I kind of scooted her arms up around my shoulders so I could put my arms around her, too. She was so much taller than me, my head was on her chest, just above her boobs. I don't think I'd ever thought about her boobs before, but they were bigger than I expected, except they were the first boobs I'd ever been near and I was feeling them with my collar bones, so who knows? Anyway, I felt like a kid being held by his mother, but it was nice. But then that changed when she leaned down and kissed me on the lips.

Our kisses had always been sitting down, so this standing kiss was a first. After I stopped worrying that she had to lean way down to kiss me, it felt great. Her mouth tasted like coffee but somehow that was exciting. I pulled a little harder with my arms around her waist to bring us even closer together. Both of my hands were on something soft behind her, and I wondered if it might be her butt, but I didn't dare move them to find out.

Then she pulled her lips away from mine and tilted her head back. It was dark, but I could tell she was looking at me. "Thank you, Wendell."

I wanted to ask her if she was still getting messages from Nokoomis or whether Reggie was now in charge. Or maybe she was still the one who was coming up with what we should do. It seemed important that I should know. But my mind went blank. Then she let me go and turned to go back to her boat.

## My Second Shelter Mission: T. Rex Comes on Board

I needed to figure out how to get Pinkie out of the shelter.

I went back to my house and got dressed like I was going to school, but instead I rode my bike back to the shelter. I walked in at 9:00 a.m. I wanted Sam and Reggie (and Nokoomis) to be proud of me.

T. Rex was surprised to see me when I walked into his storeroom in the back of the building. "Look, it's the Mop Midget, back for more fun the next day."

He looked pretty much like he did before with his ponytail covering most of the back of his uniform shirt. Underneath I could see his rock band t-shirt. He bent over a bucket, and he stood up to shake my hand. As he stood up, he had to pull his jeans up over his butt crack.

I was ready with my story. "Uh, yeah. Teachers' workshop today, no school. I figured I'd come and help you out." I wanted to flatter him right away. It was my day off from school and instead of sleeping in or screwing around with video games all day, I was there to help him, the Great T. Rex.

He bought it. We spent the next two hours (with a fifteen-minute break for two Red Bulls each) mopping crap up from the floors and refilling water and food dishes. T. Rex—or "T" as he told me to call him as we were now besties—chattered away, lecturing me on dog breeds, mop methods, and his favorite subject, how the shelter was being run into the ground by that "Total Ass-Wipe," Officer Hultz.

All the while I was listening and mopping, I tried to figure out how to get him to help me spring Pinkie Pie from the freezer.

He shared his cheese sandwich with me at eleven, and he had two more Red Bulls. I had water. My hands were still shaking from my two cans earlier. The more sugar and caffeine he had, the more he talked, but I still couldn't think of a way to bring it up.

It was back to mopping for the afternoon. Midway through, I was so tired I stopped thinking and just worked. It was all I could do.

And then we were in the storeroom at the end of the day, cleaning our mops and putting stuff away. "You tired?"

I was sitting on a bench and looked up. He hung his uniform shirt in a locker.

"Yeah." It was the truth, and I couldn't think of anything else to say.

"You act like somethin's eatin' you. You have a good time today?"

*Of course I didn't have a good time.* I mopped up dog crap and piss, but I didn't say that, and I was proud of myself. "I, uh, I just have this problem with my girlfriend."

Now, part of that was true. Sam might be my girlfriend, I didn't know, but we were kissing, that's sort of a girlfriend. And, if I didn't figure a way to get that damn pig out of there, I was really going to have a problem.

T. Rex laughed, kind of a gurgle. "Been there done that. That's why the T. flies solo."

I had to think about that for a second or two, but I think we were having a man-to-man talk about women. But from there, I didn't know what to say. So I just hung my head down and acted sad. "Yeah."

"Run it by me, maybe I can help." T. Rex sat down beside me on the bench. He had his fifth Red Bull in his hand. I wondered how he slept at night.

I just didn't know how to say it, so I figured the truth might be my only option. "Well, you won't believe it, but that pig you have in your freezer, Pinkie Pie?"

He just looked at me. And then I remembered how much he hated Officer Hultz. "That pig was my girlfriend's pet." I decided to leave out the part about the spirit grandmother. I mean, it was too weird. "Anyway, the pig was hit by a golf cart and Officer Hultz killed it with her rifle." I saw T. Rex shake his head, and I thought that was a good sign.

"My girlfriend is really upset that Hultz killed Pinkie Pie."

T. Rex nodded again.

"Anyway, my girlfriend knows there's nothing she can do to bring Pinkie Pie back, but she's upset Pinkie's going to be cremated and she won't be able to give her a proper burial."

T. Rex nodded. That was good. So I decided to just say it. "Is there any way you can help me get Pinkie out of the freezer?"

T. Rex shook his head. "I told you, Man, Hultz's got big barbeque plans for that pig. She's real pleased she killed one of the animals from the marina."

That stopped me. Hultz was even a bigger bitch than I thought. I added some stuff he'd like. "I don't want Officer Hultz to cremate her, and I want to help my girlfriend." Right at the end of what I said, I made my voice quiver. I don't know how I did it, and I'm not proud of it, but it worked.

"I don't know, Dude."

I hated to be called "Dude," but I kept quiet.

T. Rex looked down at the floor, considering. Then — suddenly — he caved. "Cremation's at two this Saturday afternoon. Be here Friday night, and I'll get you the pig."

I couldn't believe it. I jumped up and gave T. Rex a bro-hug while he was still sitting on the bench. It was awkward, but it seemed the thing to do. Then I turned to go. I wanted to get out of there before he had second thoughts. "See you Friday night."

"But, I need another pig."

I stopped in the doorway and tried to think about what he said. "*Another* pig?"

He made one of those "what-am-I-supposed-to-do?" gestures with his hands. "It's Hultz's big day. She needs a pig to cremate. I told you she's a weirdo. I need a pig to stick in your pig's place, about the same size and color."

*Frack me. This was going to be impossible.* I couldn't think of anything to say. "What time on Friday?"

"Be at the back door at ten."

As I rode my bike back across the bridge, my mind spun around in circles and honestly, I think I cried, although it might have been the wind in my eyes. *Sweet Jesus. Can this get any harder?*

I swung my bike into my driveway around five. I didn't slow down and coasted into my garage because I didn't want to see Sam.

I knew Sam would be doing chores at the marina. Thursday was the day the shrimp boat came in, and she always helped unload, but I couldn't risk her seeing me. I wanted to give her the good news—that I'd figured out a way to get Pinkie Pie out of the shelter—but that plan was all screwed up because now I had to find a replacement pig. I needed to figure it out before I talked to her.

I powered by my mom and Joel in the kitchen, and I picked up a plate of dinner on my way to my room. "Homework," I said. On the stairs, I thought about what I said and smiled. My parents would be confused. First, golf team, now I had homework.

I sat on my bed and ate my mother's meatloaf. The only thing that made my mother's meatloaf edible was ketchup, and I forgot the ketchup when I was in the kitchen. I ate it anyway. I figured I needed my strength.

I got a graph pad and pen from the table next to my bed. I needed to keep all this straight. I wrote "Wednesday night" on the top of the pad and "Friday, 10 p.m." on the bottom.

Then I wrote, "need replacement pig." And I just looked at those words for a while. Nothing came to me.

So I Googled it:

**"Pig"**

For a while I read about pigs. The genus "sus." Descendant of the wild boar. Related to the peccary and the wart hog. (Didn't know that.) Used for medical research because of similarity to humans. (That, either.)

After a while, I got tired of the history of pigs and tried out all sorts of keywords. I got more specific about what I needed:

**"Dead pig."**
**"Replacement pig."**
**"Pig cremation."**
**"Hog farm."**
**"Barbeque."**

Then my phone vibrated; it was a text from Sam:

**"My boat w/ Reggie."**

*Reggie again. Why him? What did he do?* Then I took a deep breath like one of my counselors suggested, let it out slowly, and slipped out of the house to go over to Granger's.

Sam and Reggie sat on opposite sides of the little table in Sam's cabin. Sam slid over so I could sit next to her. I felt good about that.

On the wall over her lava lamp, there was a big piece of brown wrapping paper covered with Sam's writing and drawings. Looking closer, I saw the drawings were maps.

Then I saw Reggie had a beer in front of him. I got jealous right away because I wondered how long he'd been there with Sam. I looked at it, but I didn't say anything. Then I thought about how I'd been mopping up shit all day with T. Rex, and I wondered if Sam and Reggie had done anything. I still didn't say anything.

"How was the shelter?" When Sam asked me the question, I felt her hand go onto my knee under the table. I was pretty surprised, so I didn't answer right away until she squeezed me a little. Then I remembered. I hadn't told her I was going to the shelter. I didn't even ask her how she knew. Nokoomis again.

"Uh, good. I, uh, got T. Rex to help. We need to be at the back door of the shelter at ten Friday night. We pick Pinkie up then."

Right then, Sam made a very un-Sam-like noise, sort of a little girl's giggle, and she turned to me and wrapped her arms around my neck and kissed me on the cheek. "Oh, Wendell, I'm so proud of you." And then she pulled her head away. "That's why Nokoomis sounded so happy today."

I sneaked a look at Reggie. I still didn't know if he bought this Sam-talks-to-Pinkie/Nokoomis thing. He just nodded and took a sip of his beer.

And then Sam said, "And you need a replacement pig, right?"

I just sat there. T. Rex just brought it up that afternoon. That Nokoomis was a real crystal ball.

I realized it was quiet, and Reggie and Sam were looking at me, waiting for an answer.

I straightened up in my seat and tried to sound like I knew what I was talking about. "Uh, yeah. We do. Hultz does the cremations personally, and she'll need to have some carcass that looks like Pinkie Pie." I didn't even know how the cremations worked, but I thought I sounded like an authority.

Sam asked, "What kind of vehicle are you using?"

Right then I realized Sam was a true best friend. She asked the question that way instead of "Remember, Wolf, that you're maybe the only kid in the senior class who doesn't have their driver's license? And that's because you've failed your driving test not once, not twice, but *three* times? And now you have to wait a year to take it again because you swore at the guy who was giving you the driving test after you backed into his car while you were trying to parallel park?"

If we'd been alone, she would have busted my balls like that because that's what we did. But it was different. Was it because we were kissing or because Reggie was there? Either way, things were different. I felt her hand on my bare knee. Things were very different.

## I Line up a Truck and Become a Drug Dealer

I woke up Thursday morning way before I usually did. It was still dark outside. My mind was awake even if I wasn't. I needed to be at the shelter Friday night at ten. In a vehicle big enough to carry Pinkie to the public dock on the mainland. With a replacement pig. And then I thought; *lifting*. Pinkie was 350 lbs. when she was killed. Had she gotten lighter? Did a body get heavier when it was frozen?

How many people did it take to lift 350 lbs.? Four? Five? I did the numbers in my head. I knew I sure as shit couldn't lift 75 lbs. of a frozen pig. Sweet Jesus, how were we supposed to lift a pig?

Reggie and Sam couldn't help. Sam gave me that news right after she kissed me and bit me a little on my neck. I wondered about this as I reached up and felt the bite under my ear. It was a little sore, but it was exciting. If she hadn't bitten me on the neck I might have bitched her out more about not helping load pigs at the shelter, but she had to help unload shrimp and Reggie needed to get his boat ready to pick up Pinkie. I guess those were OK reasons. Plus, there was the neck bite.

I turned on the light next to my bed and pulled the directory of students at Banyan Island High out of the bottom drawer of my desk.

When I first moved to town, I spent hours reading that directory, memorizing names and faces. Somehow I thought Florida was going to be different than Connecticut, and I was actually going to have friends. That lasted about a month until I figured out that the kids down here were pretty much the same as they were in Connecticut, so no friends for Wendell Wolf. Again. But, that didn't stop me from knowing who kids were.

I needed a kid with a truck. And a driver's license.

It didn't take me long. Banyan Island High was a small school.

I had one possibility. Jordan Minch was a Sped Shed kid, and he had a session with Ms. Gordon right after me. When she was delayed, we shot the shit. He was one of the only kids in school with a full beard. Some kids tried, but Jordan's was the real deal, full and black. I was scared of him at first, but he seemed OK with me. Plus, his dad ran a tree service. I knew Jordan worked for his dad, and maybe he could get a truck. Checking the window, I saw the sun was just coming up. I jumped out of bed and found my clothes from the night before. I needed to catch Jordan before school.

Jordan lived only a couple of streets away from me near the island's only ball field. It was easy to figure out where, because there were three trucks on the street outside a small house. The trucks all had Minch's Tree Service painted on the side.

As I cruised down his street on my bike, I wondered how I was going to explain to Jordan why I just happened to be waiting for him in front of his house. Just then, his door opened and Jordan came out, and I didn't have any more time to think up a story.

Jordan wore heavy jeans, even in the hot September weather, and he wore a T-shirt from Granger's Marina's annual fishing tournament. He had a knapsack over his shoulder, and his hair and beard were still wet from a shower. When he stepped out on the road in front of his house, I saw him take a can from the back pocket of his jeans and tuck some chewing tobacco in his mouth. This wasn't going to be easy.

He saw me on my bike and said one word, "Wolf," like it didn't surprise him I was there and was keeping up with him as he walked down the street toward school. After about ten yards, I realized we weren't going to be chatty.

"Uh, Jordan, I need your help."

He spat something on the road between us. "Doin' what?" He kept walking, and I pushed my bike along, feeling like a total dweeb.

I couldn't think of any story to tell him. I had always thought I was a pretty good liar, but I'd rushed over here and just hadn't had time to come up with a story.

"I want to hire you for a job." I don't know where that came from. I didn't have any money, but it just seemed like the thing to say to a kid like Jordan Minch.

"Doin' what?"

We had a block to go before the school so I had to talk fast. "Yeah, Sam Granger and I need to hire you to move some heavy stuff Friday night after dark."

He slowed down. "Sam Granger?"

I'd purposely mentioned Sam's name, since I guessed she probably scared him. "Yeah."

"Granger's?" Apparently, Jordan liked to say stuff twice.

"Yeah."

Looking straight ahead, he lowered his voice, even though there wasn't anyone around. "Drugs?"

My first reaction was to be pissed. How could Jordan Minch think I was dealing drugs? But luckily, I shut up. It was a good story.

I tried to look guilty. "Yeah. Drugs."

He looked skeptical. "*You're* dealing?"

How could I convince him? "Uh, yeah, uh, not all the time, this is just a special…deal." I watched him to see if he bought it. He looked just as numb as usual.

So I pretended to get a phone call.

"Uh, yeah." (Pause, like someone on the other end was speaking.) "Yeah, Friday." (Pause) Out of the corner of my eye, I watched Jordan. He was listening. "Uh, yeah. Good quality stuff." I thought fast. What did they say in movies? "Uh, *primo.*" Sweet Jesus that sounded lame. *Primo.* But I glanced at Jordan and he was nodding. "OK." I made a big show of clicking off the phone and nodding like I was a Mexican drug lord.

It worked. Jordan's lips barely moved. "$100. Cash. Up front."

"Will you be able to lift a heavy load?"

I thought I saw him smirk. "No problem."

Again I thought about the money I didn't have, but if I got it, I'd have Jordan's truck.

"OK."

Back at the house, I went in through the garage. I had an idea where I could find the money I needed. I stood in back of Joel's fancy golf cart and unzipped the big compartment on the side of his golf bag, all the while listening for footsteps on the stairs. I reached in and there it was, mixed in with Joel's balls and tees and all the other crap he had in there. I pulled it out and held it up to the light. A wad of money. I squinted. Twenties, a bunch of them!

I always figured Joel gambled when he golfed. One night I heard Joel tell someone on the phone to bring cash to their golf game. I'd stored away that info in case I ever needed some fast money. I figured it would be in his bag. I took the whole stash. He wouldn't suspect me, he'd just think he was drunk and lost it on a bet.

## We Go to the Inn

I went upstairs to my bedroom and dressed for school. I heard the garage door go up and Joel take off in his cart. I felt pretty good. Now I had a truck, Jordan Minch's help, and some cash. That was for about thirty seconds until I remembered I needed a replacement pig. I needed to substitute the new pig for Pinkie, steal Pinkie out of the animal shelter, and get him to the public landing. That put me in a bad mood.

My phone vibrated in the pocket of my shorts and I got a text from Sam:

**"Meet me at picnic table at 8:30. Going to Inn."**

Now my bad mood turned into confusion. I checked the time: *8:00 a.m.* What about school?

So, I stood by the picnic table and waited where Sam told me to. I didn't know why I couldn't just knock on the cabin door, but…you know, Sam told me to wait there.

The cabin door opened, and Sam came up the stairs from down below. The first thing I saw was her hair. Instead of hanging loose, her hair was braided in back and somehow it was on top of her head. I know that sounds stupid, but it was nice. The next thing I saw was the dress. It wasn't her dress; it was a dress like all the women my mother's age wore, all flowers with bright colors. I knew there was a shop in town that sold dresses like that. *Lily Something*. When Sam finally got to the top of the stairs, I could see the whole thing. It was a short dress, and I could see a lot of her dark legs. She had on one of her sparkly Calusa necklaces, the one made of cat's-paw shells. On her feet she wore these little sandals.

She stepped off the boat onto the dock and smiled at me

I smiled back as she walked up. "Very pretty." I knew I was supposed to say something, but it was true. Sam was beautiful. She wasn't the usual Sam, but she was still beautiful. She seemed a little embarrassed.

"Thank you," she said, her voice quieter than usual.

She pointed back to her boat. "There are some clothes in there for you to wear." I started to object, but I caught myself. Sam was all dressed up. The least I could do…I guess I was learning.

On her bed, I found a jacket on a pink hangar with some other stuff. I recognized the hangar; the clothes came from Banyan Bargains. I really didn't want to get dressed in other people's clothes. I know that sounds weird, but that's what Banyan Bargains was all about. The rich people did it, why shouldn't I?

I put everything on and I looked in the mirror on Sam's closet door. I had on:

1. A white dress shirt with some sort of monogram on the pocket.
2. A pair of really ironed khakis with a belt that had jumping fish on it.
3. A blue sport coat made of some kind of cloth that had little bumps in it. I checked the label sewn on the inside pocket. It came from some fancy men's shop in Sarasota.
4. And these little baby-blue slipper/loafers that looked like a girl's.

Everything fit. How did Sam know my size?

When I met Sam by the picnic table, she smiled but didn't say anything. I was happy about that. I felt stupid. I didn't need any comments.

She turned and started to walk toward my house. "Are your parents home?"

I actually felt my heart jump. *Why did Sam want to know that? More kissing?* I knew Joel was gone. I checked the garage. My mom's Prius was gone. "No. Why?"

"We need Joel's car."

First, I was disappointed. No kissing. Then I was so shocked I stopped right in the street. I couldn't move or talk. Finally I got my feet and mouth to move as I ran after her. To her back, I stammered, "The Escalade?" Then, "Why?"

When she got to the car, she just opened the door and got in the driver's seat. Even as big as she was, she had to pull herself up. The

Escalade is like an SUV on steroids. It's the kind of car you see rappers and professional sports people driving. There was no reason for Joel to have a car like that on Banyan Island, except for one thing; everyone else had one.

I heard the Escalade start, and I ran to the passenger side. Maybe I couldn't drive, but Sam could—of course, she passed her driver's test on the first try. She drove all sorts of cars, trucks, and equipment over at Granger's.

I was clicking my seat belt as she backed to the bottom of the driveway. "How long is your father going to be gone?"

" 'Til dinner." That was true, but it still didn't keep me from looking around to see if any of the neighbors were watching.

She smiled her smile that meant she knew something I didn't. "Great."

Sam parked in the circle outside the Inn, just like everybody else. She turned the engine off and began to get out until I stopped her. "Wait."

She looked over at me.

"Why are we here at the Inn?" Joel's frigging Escalade was right outside the Inn in the circle. I didn't think it was a stupid question, but I forgot to ask earlier, I was so excited about going somewhere with Sam all dressed-up.

Sam slammed her door and waited for me in front of the hood. "We need to look comfortable here so we can scout the place out after breakfast. They only serve breakfast for another half hour. Then we have an appointment with Pugsley."

I kind of saw stars and got dizzy. Breakfast? Scouting around? And the worst: Pugsley?

Pugsley was a big deal on Banyan Island. I think his first name was "Dennis," but everybody called him Pugsley. He had his picture in the paper all the time. And Joel was always talking about Pugsley. "Pugsley did this and Pugsley said that." He didn't say these things to me, of course, but to my mom. I just had to hear his shit.

When Joel heard I went to see Pugsley without telling him, he'd give me shit. Like I need another reason for him to give me crap.

We were on the sidewalk.

"But…?" (Me)

"Just go with it." (Sam)

We walked up the polished wooden stairs, and Sam took my arm just like we were on a date or something. It felt good, but I was still really nervous. How would two high school kids look walking around this old place?

The hotel front desk was inside the front door with two ladies behind it. Both of them said good morning. I guess nobody snuck in here.

Sam spoke up, "Good morning. We're here for the buffet." The ladies nodded like Sam said what she was supposed to.

We had to go through a big open room to get to the dining room, and I guess Sam knew the way because I felt her guiding me with her hand under my arm. By that time I could smell bacon, so I knew we were going the right way. I love bacon. (Sorry, Pinkie!)

The big room was filled with really colorful couches and chairs and lots of old people sitting around reading newspapers and books. Some of the old guys were even sleeping. There were Inn workers everywhere, polishing, vacuuming, and picking up cups and dishes.

Then we got to the dining room where there was another old lady at a stand-up desk. Sam walked right up to her and started talking. "Good morning. Two for the breakfast buffet, please."

The lady looked down at a notebook in front of her. "Do you have reservations?"

Sam smiled. "No, we do not."

I felt a burning sensation in my chest.

"Are you a guest of the hotel?"

I felt my face get hot. I knew coming here was a stupid thing to do. Hultz was in charge of security at the Inn. They'll call her and the school and my parents, and we're screwed. I think I took a step backwards, and I felt Sam squeeze my arm hard. And it hurt.

"No, we're here for a meeting with Mr. Pugsley. We'd like a table for two please, by the window, if possible."

I remember trying to breathe. Sam actually asked for a table by the window.

The lady just looked at Sam and smiled. She waved at someone, and a waiter came over. He smiled at us and held out his hand, "This way please." His accent was Caribbean, but it was different than Reggie's. As we walked between the tables, I checked out the other people. All of them were old, about the same age as my mom and Joel.

We got to this table by the window that looked like it was made of bamboo, and it had two really big chairs with red and yellow flowers on the huge cushions. The waiter pulled back one of the chairs and stood behind it. I didn't know what to do, but I was closest so I started to sit down. Then Sam really squeezed my arm, and I think I flinched. I checked my arm the next day, and she'd left fingerprint bruises. Anyway, she pulled me back, stepped in front of me and sat down. The waiter slid the chair in under her butt, and she smoothed her skirt just like she knew what she was doing. I waited a second to see if he was going to do the same thing with my chair, but then I hurried and sat down without him.

And then, I felt something in my lap that shouldn't be there and I jumped. The waiter actually put this big cloth napkin in my lap for me. That was so strange.

"Uh…." I almost said something, but Sam rescued me.

"We'll have coffee, please, Jean Claude, and we are going to have the buffet."

The waiter got this really friendly smile and said, "Very good, Miss Granger." Then he looked at me. "How are you, today, Mr. Wolf?" I tried to answer, but all I could do was make a squeaking noise. As he walked away, I must not have looked very good because Sam said, "Take five deep breaths, Wendell. Keep smiling. You'll be OK in a minute."

I did what she said and all the stuff I was feeling—a combination of puking, running away or fainting—began to go away. I started to use the napkin to wipe my forehead, but then I put it back in my lap, pretty sure I wasn't supposed to do that. I used my fingers instead.

"How did the waiter know our names?" I looked around to see if anyone was listening.

Sam smiled. "He's a friend of Reggie's. Reggie texted him and told him to watch out for us."

I couldn't help myself. I felt angry again. *Was this all Reggie's idea? What happened to Pinkie Pie's ideas?* And then I stopped. I couldn't believe I was hoping to get ideas from the dead pig. I focused on the table to calm down. There were more utensils than I had ever seen. There were tiny little jars of jelly and honey. I wondered, if you used part of a jar, would they let you take the rest home? I felt a little better.

Jean Claude was back with our coffee in a little silver pot and poured each of us a cup. "A Coca-Cola for you, Mr. Wolf?"

*How did he know that?* I just nodded.

"Very good, Sir." And he walked away.

I tried to ask Sam about it, but she stood up. "Let's go to the buffet."

I had been to the buffets before, Pizza Hut and salad bars, but this was something else. They had everything anyone would ever want for breakfast all laid out on tables along the wall. The hot stuff was in pans with little fires under them. As we got close, Sam whispered, "Do what I do, take what I take."

She started at the first table and picked up this small plate and put fruit on it, blueberries, raspberries, and some kind of melon. Then she turned to go back to our table by the window. I followed, but I wasn't happy. *All that food and we were only having fruit? I wanted bacon.*

Back at the table, Sam said the fruit was only a starter plate, which was good because I really didn't like fruit much. I was done in about thirty seconds, even though Sam told me to slow down. Then Sam stood up again and motioned for me to follow her back to the buffet. I grabbed my plate and followed. Suddenly, Jean Claude stepped in from the side and snuck the plate out of my hand. "You get a new plate, Sir." Then he smiled like he and I had a secret. "I take this one."

By the time I got through the line, I had something on my plate from every pan or platter. I took ten strips of bacon, even after Sam told me to go easy. The one thing I didn't take was grits. I hate grits.

It was the best breakfast I had ever eaten:

1. Coke
2. Fruit

3. Scrambled eggs
4. Hash browns
5. Bagel with cream cheese
6. 10 Bacon strips
7. Sausages
8. French toast (with syrup)
9. Three sweet rolls
10. Four small jelly jars (hidden in pocket to go home)

After I started to eat and it didn't look like we were going to get thrown out, I began to enjoy myself. Sam put her fork down on her plate (she only had half the food I did) and patted her lips with her big napkin. Then she folded it and put it back in her lap. The table had a glass top, and I could see her legs and her short dress. She caught me looking.

I thought she'd be pissed, but she kind of smiled and then she winked. I don't know why, but I really liked that. A girl never winked at me before.

She lowered her voice. "Nokoomis says there might be a replacement pig in the Inn. After we see Pugsley, we need to walk around like tourists and find it."

I put my fork down and just looked at her. *Nokoomis again?* I started to say something, and then I remembered all the stuff Nokoomis had been right about: the shell mounds, the cremation date, and that we were going to need a replacement pig. For like the one-hundredth time, I wondered if it was Nokoomis coming up with this stuff, or was it Sam? Or now, even Reggie. Those thoughts went by real quickly. But I didn't say anything.

Jean Claude arrived at the table with a small leather folder, handed it to me and walked away. I opened it and almost threw up. It was the bill for breakfast, and I'd forgot my wallet. I didn't have any money. *Wasn't the guy supposed to pay the bill? Shit.*

Then I read it. $25 each for the buffet, plus tax. But down at the bottom, someone had written, "No charge, tip included." I looked over at Sam, and she was smiling. She probably knew what it said. Our breakfast was free. Reggie again, but this was good. I started to breathe again and stood up. Before Jean Claude could get there, I got to the back of Sam's chair and pulled it out for her. She took my arm as we left the room and it felt great.

I don't know how she set up the appointment with Pugsley, but I think she called and said she was from some community group awards committee. Of course Pugsley fell for it. That was the kind of shit he was into.

We walked back down this really thick carpet to the lobby and up to the front desk. Sam went up to the same lady she'd talked to before. "We have an appointment with Mr. Pugsley at ten."

"I'll get him for you, Ma'am. Won't you have a seat here in the lobby? May I get you anything while you wait?" I looked around because I was nervous about seeing Joel. He was golfing, but there was always a chance he could come in there.

"I don't think so. We'll just sit here and wait." She looked around. "I'll just peruse this issue of Town and Country." She sat down on this white wicker couch and picked up a magazine from a table.

*"Peruse?"* I almost laughed out loud. I couldn't believe Sam actually said "peruse."

"I'll tell Mr. Pugsley you're here, Ma'am." The woman hurried back down the hall.

Pugsley met us at his office door and shook our hands. I thought he held Sam's hand longer than he needed to, but I might have imagined that.

Pugsley was one of those adults who tried to be super-cool by being so smooth. He must have known we were two high school kids, I mean he had to know I was Joel Wolf's son. Instead, he played it like we were actual town people there for a business meeting.

He and I were pretty much dressed alike, except his clothes looked like they were made for him while mine felt like a costume. He had on a blue sport coat with shiny gold buttons, and he had a yellow silk handkerchief in his front pocket, sticking out like he just stuffed it in there. Instead of little slippers like mine, his shoes were white leather with gold buckles. And he didn't have on any socks.

"It's nice of you to come in." That's what he said as he pointed to two chairs in front of his desk, as he sat in the one behind it. He said that like he was happy we were there. Total bullshit.

His office was filled with all kinds of stuff and pictures all arranged to make him seem like a big deal. There were pictures on the wall with him and important people like former presidents. There was a set of golf clubs in the corner.

On the wall there was a rack of fishing rods and behind him a giant tarpon hung on the wall. (There are "stuffed" tarpon hung up all over town. In Florida Culture class, we learned that you can't even pull a tarpon out of the water when you catch it. You reel it up to the boat and cut the line. Then you go someplace and get a plastic model made of the fish you imagined you might have caught. Stupid, huh?) Anyway, Pugsley had a huge plastic tarpon model with some kind of hook with feathers on it hanging out of its mouth.

Pugsley sat behind his desk and looked right at Sam. "How may I be of service?"

I was a little pissed. I mean, I was there, too, wasn't I? On the other hand, Sam knew what to say and I didn't, so Pugsley was looking in the right direction.

"Thank you for seeing us." Sam gave him one of her incredible smiles that, of course, made me jealous. It also made me wonder. I didn't know Sam could smile like that when she didn't really mean it.

She reached in the folder she carried, pulled out a folded map, carefully unfolded it, and spread it out on top of Pugsley's desk. Then she stood up and began pointing to things on the map.

"It has recently come to our attention there is a sacred Calusa burial ground under the Big Banyan." I could tell Sam had practiced that opening line. She leaned over and pointed to the map.

Pugsley shoved his chair back and stood up. He leaned over, supposedly to see where Sam was pointing. "Hmmm," he said like he was interested.

"The reason we are here is to request that the Inn allow us to use the shell mound under the Big Banyan as a burial ground and conduct a Calusa funeral there this Saturday."

I watched Pugsley's face for a reaction. He was good. You don't manage the most important place in a town of rich people by not being a pro, but I swear his face twitched. He probably couldn't control it, his right cheek jerked upward toward his eye. Just a little. He must have felt it, because he rubbed his face with his hand. I noticed his fingernails were all shiny.

He sat back down in his chair, and Sam sat back down in hers. There was silence as he made a little tent out of his hands. He looked at the ceiling. Finally, he spoke. "Certainly, the Inn values its role in preserving the history of the island."

He paused and looked at Sam and, for the first time, at me. Without controlling it, I smiled because I was so happy he looked at me. *God, I'm so pathetic.*

"But, the Calusas were wide-spread in this part of Florida. There are established, acknowledged shell mounds on other area islands. Have you considered those?"

He looked at Sam with this sincere, open-eyed look. It was so good, he got me. I even wondered why we weren't doing this on another island.

Sam was quick. "Calusa custom is to bury the deceased as close as possible to where they lived their life here on Earth."

I glanced at her out of the corner of my eye. I thought this might be bullshit, a thought I frequently had when Sam talked about the Calusas. I never knew if it was Calusa Custom or Sam's Custom.

"You're aware of course, that we are hosting the Heritage Day dinner here at the Inn this Saturday?"

Sam was prepared for this. "Yes. If you allow the burial it would include the Calusas as part of Banyan's history instead of just pirates."

I could tell Pugsley thought about that. He was probably trying to figure out how to make some money off the idea. Then: "I'm afraid it's not possible." He said it quietly, like it was a Supreme Court decision.

All of a sudden, Pugsley was standing. "Thank you for coming in. It was a pleasure to meet the two of you." He stuck his hand out to me. "You're Joel's son, aren't you? I see the resemblance."

That douche. He must have known I was adopted. Joel tells

everybody. There's no way he wouldn't have blabbed it to Pugsley, a guy he's trying to impress. How his son is so fragged up because he's from Russia, blah, blah, blah. There wasn't any resemblance and he knew it.

"I'll be sure to tell him you visited." Was that a threat? I didn't know.

"Yeah." It was all I could think to say. Without knowing how it happened, we were in the hall outside Pugsley's office with him saying meaningless shit. "Nice to visit. Good to see you. Good luck. Worthy cause."

Wow. That ended quickly.

We went down the big hallway in the middle of the Inn. I was still thinking about Pugsley, but Sam looked at everything. "Keep your eyes open, act like we belong here," she said. I thought she should be more pissed off about the way Pugsley treated us, but it didn't seem to bother her.

We passed a glass case filled with shells that people had found with little labels on each one. From there, we moved down the hall, and Sam stopped at each picture on the wall and studied it. Most of them were of old people with huge fish. Continuing down the hall, we had to step around a maid dusting the walls. Then we stopped in a room where they had coffee and sweet rolls and more old guys sleeping in their chairs. Finally, I couldn't take it anymore. It didn't seem like we were doing anything, and I thought about someone recognizing Joel's Escalade out front. I leaned toward Sam and whispered, "What are we *doing*?"

Sam pulled me out of that room. "I told you. Nokoomis said there might be a replacement pig in the Inn."

Now that I had seen what the Inn was like inside, it seemed even stupider to me. "But…."

We kept going down the hall. Finally, at the end we came to a room where I could see a pool table. Above the door was a stuffed fish, and there was a sign that said "Trophy Room."

Inside there were two guys playing pool, and Sam gave them a "Good morning" like she belonged there. The room was kind of dark and dusty, and I looked around. There were stuffed fish all over the place on the walls. At the end of the room over the pool table, there was a huge stuffed alligator on a shelf with its mouth open and teeth showing.

Then I felt Sam give my arm a squeeze, and she tilted her head toward the other end of the room. There was rock fireplace, and all around it there were stuffed animals on shelves. The first one was a bobcat with sharp teeth. Above it was a big turtle—a Gopher Tortoise, the sign under it said. And then I saw it on the mantel, high over the fireplace, a stuffed wild pig.

I told you we learned a lot about plants and animals in my Florida Culture class, so I knew about wild pigs. They're called boars, and they look a little like regular pigs, but they are skinnier and have taller legs. Most of them have tusks, too, these little horns sticking out under their mouths. People in Florida hunt boars, which I guess was why Sam and I were staring at a stuffed one.

I couldn't believe it. Nokoomis was right. There was a stupid pig in the Inn. Then I looked closer. "It's not big enough." I whispered it to Sam. It really wasn't, it must have been a baby boar, maybe a teenager.

"Shhh." I saw her look over her shoulder at the guys playing pool to see if they were watching.

Then, she got up on this rock bench in front of the fireplace, stretched and grabbed the boar's leg and gave it a tug. At first, I watched her dress go up the back of her legs, but then I jerked my head back to the pool players. I could see the commotion if Sam pulled that pig down from the mantel. But, they were pretty busy with their game.

The boar didn't move. Sam whispered, "It's nailed or glued down."

"I think you should get down from there." I whispered it to Sam.

"Do you think they'd notice it if it was gone?" It was a good question from Sam. She was still on that bench thing.

I looked around. There were animals lined up on the shelf all around the room, but where the boar was seemed like a big deal, right over the fireplace. I thought of all those people we saw working in the rest of the hotel, dusting and polishing. "Yeah, I think someone would notice."

"Yeah," Sam agreed.

"And, it's too small," I said again, thinking of Officer Hultz and how we needed another pig around Pinkie's size.

Sam let go of the boar's leg, jumped down, grabbed my hand and pulled me toward the door to the hall. "OK, Nokoomis had another idea."

*Great.* I felt that big breakfast roll over in my stomach.

## We Search for a Replacement Pig

Leaving the Inn, Sam pulled Joel's Escalade onto the road, but she turned away from my house and the marina. "No…." I started to say something, but she was ready and she just waved like I was supposed to shut up.

As she drove she reached into the top of her dress, pulled out a folded piece of paper, and handed it to me. I just sat there with the paper in my hand. It was damp. S*he must have had it in her bra! Did girls' breasts sweat?*

It smelled a little like baby powder. I wanted to hold it up to my nose, but I thought that would look perverted.

Sam glanced over and, luckily, I didn't think she knew what I was thinking about. "Open it. Reggie drew me a map."

Even though I had only lived in Florida for a year, I'm pretty good with maps. I could see right away we were going off the island.

Most people only know Florida because of its beaches, that and Disney, right? But if you head away from the beach for an hour, it's like a cowboy show. There are all these farms and horses and cows. They even have rodeos in Florida.

Reggie wrote something on the map, and I tried to read his handwriting. *Ken's* ____ I squinted at the second word, which wasn't easy with Sam driving like she was in a race. "Rendering." "Ken's Rendering." I looked over at Sam. "What's rendering?"

She shrugged. I didn't feel so bad. If Sam didn't know, I shouldn't know. She's from Florida and she's smart.

We were supposed to take a right on a little road on the map, and I pointed it out to Sam. We were nowhere, a total dusty dirt road with nothing on it. And then I saw the smokestacks coming up and a big chain link fence. The sign on the fence said "Ken's Rendering." I still didn't know what rendering was, but this place didn't look like where we should be.

Sam pulled right up to a guard booth outside the front gate. A sweaty fat guy in a tan uniform came out of the booth with a clipboard. By this time, Sam had opened her window.

"Hep ya?"

Right then, through Sam's open window, I smelled it. The place stunk, whatever it was.

"Yes, we're looking for a dead pig." Leave it to Sam to come right out with it.

The guard gave her a weird look, but he didn't say anything.

"We're looking for a dead pig?" This time Sam said it like a question.

"Say again?" The guard finally figured out something to say.

Sam turned and motioned to me. "My associate, Wendell Wolf, and I need to purchase a dead pig." The guard stepped closer and looked through the open window at me. I sunk down in my seat. With Sam in her flowered dress and me in my Banyan Bargains outfit, I'm sure we looked stupid.

"You're kidding, right?" The guard took his hat off and rubbed sweat off his bald head.

"No, I am completely serious." Sam had her most serious look on her face.

Now I felt the sweat pouring down my back under my shirt.

Sam's voice was louder when she spoke. "Look, *Vincent.* (It was on his nametag) We're just two people looking for a dead pig. Somebody told us that you had them here. Are you going to just stand there all day shooting the shit or are you going to help us?"

Vincent the guard took a step back. He wasn't used to big, beautiful dark-skinned girls talking to him that way, or any way at all, I guess. "Uh, we got pigs, but we don't sell 'em, we just grind 'em."

That shut both of us up.

All of a sudden there was a honking coming from a trailer truck driving up from behind us.

Vincent pointed down at the pavement. "You need to get off the scale. This guy's always in a hurry."

Sam moved the Escalade off to the side of the guard booth. This old truck pulled up where we were parked, and the driver handed a clipboard down to Vincent. He went inside the booth, looked at something, wrote something on the clipboard, came back, and handed it up to the driver. Without a word, the driver gunned the truck engine and pulled away, leaving an incredible stink of dead animal, diesel fuel, and dust. As his trailer went past us, we saw various animal legs and other body parts sticking out the top and sides. And it stunk.

Sam pulled the Escalade back in front of the guard booth and rolled down her window. Vincent had turned to go back in his little air-conditioned office, but he stopped and looked irritated that we were back.

Sam leaned out her window. "What's rendering?"

He tipped his hat back a little on his head and answered. "We grind up and boil dead animals. Use 'em for fertilizer, pet food, that kind of thing."

I leaned over Sam and asked him, "So we can't buy a dead pig here?"

Now he looked mad again. "Look, I don't know who sent you here in your fancy clothes in your daddy's Caddy, but you had your fun. Now get the fig off my scale and leave me alone."

Sam spewed gravel out behind us when she turned from the gravel road onto the highway.

"We've got to get Joel's car back before he gets home." I said it quietly so it wouldn't irritate her.

Sam just shrugged and didn't say anything, but I noticed she speeded up. Now I was worried about being pulled over by cops. I started to think about how to explain Joel's car theft to him.

And then I thought about the replacement pig again. First the Inn and then Ken's Rendering. Two dead ends. Maybe Nokoomis wasn't that smart.

Sam was quiet as she drove, and I found a back road on the map on my phone that looked like it would be faster going back than the way we came. It was a tiny two-lane road that went straight for like ten miles. On either side of us there were orange groves, and I rolled my window down to let in the sweet fruity smell. Except for the fact that Sam had tears rolling down her face and I was going to be grounded for five years for taking Joel's Escalade and we couldn't find a replacement pig, it might have been fun to be there.

I felt bad for Sam because she was crying, but I also wanted her to slow down because we were going like 90 mph along that little road.

"What does Nokoomis think of this?" I know. It was a stupid thing to say. I was getting better, but stuff like that still slipped out.

She took her eyes off the road and gave me a sideways look. "You don't ask Nokoomis questions like a fortune teller, Wolf." And then she speeded up.

She was back to calling me "Wolf." I hoped that didn't mean our kissing was going to stop.

"How do you get information from her?" That was also a stupid question, but I was trying to get back on her good side. But her driving fast made me nervous and I was already nervous about my stupid question about Nokoomis.

Instead of getting even more pissed, Sam just sighed and another tear rolled down her cheek. I wanted to lean over and wipe it off, but I was too far away in that giant Escalade, plus I was still holding onto the door handle because she was now—I snuck a peek at the speedometer—doing 95 mph.

Then I saw something dark flash by on my side of the road, and I remember smelling something bad through my open window. It took me a second or two to connect what I saw to my brain. I couldn't believe it.

"Stop!" I didn't mean to yell it, but I guess I did, because Sam jammed on the brakes. Hard. We stopped with a lot of tire screeching and bumping. The back end of the Escalade came around, but we stopped. Right in the middle of the road.

Sam looked at me with her eyes huge and at least she wasn't crying anymore. Instead of being sad, she was pissed.

"What the heck?"

Though Sam doesn't say "heck."

My seat belt carved a groove in my shoulder when we stopped, and I unbuckled it. I turned around in my seat to look out the back window. "Back up."

Sam slammed the Escalade into reverse and laid rubber backing up. I didn't know you could do that.

We were going so fast we almost missed it. "Stop," I shouted, but not as loud as last time. Sam stopped, but not as hard as last time.

I opened my door and jumped out. The first thing I noticed was the smell, the rotten stink I smelled before. There was also the sweet smell of the orange grove, and the combination of fruit and rotten smell made my stomach roll. Between the big breakfast, the rendering place and Sam's racecar driving, my stomach wasn't so great, anyhow.

Sam came around the front of the Escalade, and we stood there together and looked.

It was a wild boar—a dead wild boar—on its back by the side of the road. I knew I saw something. Actually, you see them every now and then, cars hit them and then leave them dead by the side of the road. I should have remembered that.

The boar made me think of Pinkie after she got hit by the golf cart, because all four of its legs were in the air, although Pinkie's legs were swirling around and this pig's legs were frozen stiff, straight up.

It was a full-grown boar, its stomach was really swollen, and there were flies all over it. That's where the smell was coming from.

"This must be why Nokoomis sent us out here."

I looked at Sam to see if she was making a joke, but I knew she wasn't. She really believed.

We stood there and looked at the stiff pig. I glanced up and down the road. There was nothing coming either way. We were really out in the country.

Then I heard a squawk somewhere above, and a shadow passed between Sam and me. There were turkey vultures circling. Turkey vultures are these huge ugly black birds they have in Florida that eat road kill. I wondered if we'd scared them away from their lunch.

Have you ever loaded a dead, stiff, rotten wild boar into the back of a Cadillac Escalade? I'm thinking probably not. It's not easy.

We got the Escalade's back gate up and backed it over right next to the boar. I looked up to see if the buzzards would be angry and try to dive bomb us, but they just kept flying around.

The flies and the stink and the buzzards and the heat made me move fast. Sam took charge. "OK, grab the legs on the other side." I reached out and grabbed the boar's hairy ankles. Sam did the same.

"On three. One, two, THREE!" We lifted and heaved at the same time. It didn't work. First, the Escalade is a really tall car, so getting something heavy up into the back is hard. Second, I'm a weakling. Sam got her side a little off the ground, but I couldn't move mine.

Sam took a big breath. "OK, try again."

I didn't have any hope a second try would be any different.

"One, two, THREE." We both heaved and grunted. Again, nothing.

I could really taste my breakfast in my throat now, especially all that bacon. I was sweating and the stench was awful and I think I pulled a muscle in my chest trying to lift that boar.

From far away, we heard a loud truck and it came closer.

Two Cuban farm workers drove up in an old tricked out pick-up truck. Their exhaust made a lot of noise. Their pick-up was loaded with oranges, and the guys got out and walked up to us.

Sam and I were behind the Escalade, and the boar was still on the ground. Both of us were sweaty and gross, even in our nice clothes. Of course I was scared. I tried to figure out how to hide what we were doing, but it was pretty obvious, so I just stood there.

The Cubans just stood there, looking. Finally, Sam said something in Spanish and she started to laugh. Then they began to laugh. I know I gave Sam a weird look. I didn't know she spoke Spanish, but I didn't want to be left out, so I laughed, too.

Then we all stopped, and Sam said something to them. The driver ran to the back of his pick-up and came back with an old blanket. Sam took it and spread it in the back of the Escalade. When she did this, her skirt went up the backs of her legs, and one of the Cuban guys whistled. When Sam turned around, she said something and they all laughed. I was jealous, and I was tired of getting left out of the conversation. Then the Cubans reached down and grabbed the stupid dead boar by two legs and Sam and I grabbed the other two and we swung it back and forth a couple of times and chucked it up into the Escalade. It was pretty easy with four people.

Sam reached in her bra and pulled out a twenty and offered it to the guys and they said no, but the three of them laughed some more. Then one of the guys went back to their truck and came back with a crate of oranges and he shoved it in the Escalade next to the boar.

Then he held his nose and pointed to the Escalade. I guess he thought the oranges would cut the stink from the pig. He was wrong.

It was a two-hour ride back to the island. We rode with all the windows open and the Escalade's air conditioning going full blast. The crate of oranges smelled orange-y, but it wasn't enough to beat the smell of the dead boar. There were like a million flies in there, and while Sam drove, I waved as many as I could out the open window.

"What are we going to do with the boar?" It was the obvious question and even though I didn't have an answer, I was happy Sam asked me instead of telling me she heard from Nokoomis, Reggie, or even that she had an idea herself.

I didn't have an answer so I just started talking. "I need to have the replacement pig at the shelter at ten tomorrow night." This wasn't big news. We both knew it. "So…." I drew the word out, like I was thinking.

After about a minute of silence, Sam said, "So...what?

Shit. I liked Sam relying on me, but I really didn't know what to do. "Maybe we can take it to the shelter early." I came up with this, but I knew it wasn't a very good idea.

Sam sounded excited. "Do you think that would work?"

"Uh, now that I think about it, I'd need to find T. Rex, and he'd need to let us in, and then there'd be an extra pig in the freezer which wouldn't match Officer Hultz's inventory if she came around. No, I don't think that would work."

Sam stopped at a light. We left the little road and now we were on the highway headed to the island. We didn't have a plan for the pig or an excuse for stealing Joel's car. I started to feel sick, and it wasn't the rotten pig.

Then it came to me: "Uh, Jordan Minch."

Sam looked over. "A loser. Why bring him up?"

I tried to think of a way to make it sound better than it was. "Uh, he's part of my…team….he's going to help with the…transfer of… Pinkie, uh, tomorrow night."

"What?"

I felt defensive, and I was embarrassed that we had a dead pig in the back of Joel's car and I didn't know what to do with it. "Look. You and that frigging Reggie put me in charge of getting frigging Pinkie Pie out of the shelter, and I figured out a way. Why are you giving me shit about it?" I stopped. This was the way we used to talk to each other before the kissing began.

Everything was quiet in the car. The wind from the open windows blew her dress up her legs, and even though her dress and her legs were dirty from hoisting the boar, they still looked nice.

She took one of her hands off the steering wheel and reached over and took my hand. It felt good even though her driving the Escalade with one hand made me nervous. And she had dead boar germs on her hand.

"Sorry, Wendell. I know you've got a good plan. Tell me what we need to do."

It was still light when we made it to Jordan's. Sam took the long way around the island so we didn't get anywhere near my house. For the past hour, I'd been getting texts from my mother about the fact that neither I—nor Joel's Escalade—were home. I was pretty sure she'd connected the two, and I knew I was in serious trouble.

In front of Jordan's, Sam turned off the engine and right away, the boar smell was on us like a cloud. I jumped out my side and went up to Jordan's door.

He pushed open his screen door, saw me, squinted out to the street, and saw Sam and the Escalade. "What? Thought you said tomorrow night."

I just started talking, trying to sound like an improvising—but still in *total* control—drug dealer. "Uh, yeah, Jordan. We need you to take care of the….package a little early."

As I think I mentioned, Jordan Minch was not the brightest bulb on the tree, but you could tell he was going to be good in business. "That's gonna cost an extra $20."

"Fine." I was OK with this. I had a stinking, fly-covered boar in the back of my father's car that I was in deep shit for stealing, so I needed to hurry. I took the money out of my wallet. "Here."

Sam and I helped Jordan and his two brothers pull the dead boar out of the Escalade, and then we wrapped it in this huge tarp they used for carrying leaves and other shit around in their tree business. A couple of times, I had to tell Jordan that the dead pig was key in the drug deal he was counting on. He bought it.

Jordan's yard was a mess. There was broken-down machinery everywhere and piles of all sorts of stuff. There were three or four big chickens running around. We weighted the tarp down with cement blocks next to a big mound of fertilizer. From the road you couldn't tell if the smell was coming from the rotten boar or the pile of manure.

Sam and I took Joel's Escalade back to the marina. Sam was still in her flowered dress, but she crawled in the back of the SUV with a big spray bottle of Febreze.

I used a scrub brush and soap and water. Sam used a sponge and all sorts of boat cleaners. We worked on it for almost an hour. It still stunk. Every time we tried a different cleaner, we'd walk away, then walk back and sniff. Every time, it still stunk. Finally, we gave up. Maybe the smell was going away, or maybe we were just used to it. But we were tired and we gave up.

Sam drove the Escalade across the street from the marina to our driveway. Before she turned it off, she rolled down all the windows. I walked her down to the end of our driveway, and she kissed me and I held her in that nice dress which was a mess, but still nice. Both of us smelled really bad. "Good luck. Come over later," she said and gently turned me toward my house.

On my way into the house, I thought about how I was going to explain the missing— and stinking—Escalade to Joel. I thought up a story where we had to take one of Sam's goats on an emergency visit to a special veterinary clinic. That could explain the smell. It wasn't a great story, but it was all I had.

I thought through what I'd find inside. The kitchen and family room in our house was one big open room. Dinner was a couple of hours ago. Joel would be in front of the wide-screen TV at the far end, in his chair watching the Golf Channel. My mother would be on a stool at the counter in the kitchen on her computer.

I was ready with my story, I really was, but Joel was asleep in his chair. It was later than I planned.

I stood behind him. "I'm sorry, Joel. You see, Sam had this sick goat and we needed to get him to a clinic—a special goat clinic." And then I stopped. It didn't matter if I had a good excuse. I was tired, he was asleep. They were going to ground me and take away my "privileges"—whatever they were—no matter what I said. So I crossed the room and headed to the stairs.

"Sorry doesn't cut it." Joel sounded pretty groggy. Right away, I flashed on a thought that he wouldn't remember this conversation, but I decided he would, especially when he smelled his Escalade.

As I walked up the stairs, I heard angry whispering between Joel and my mom. I heard the words "do something about him"—but I'd heard that a million times.

## We Plan Some More With Reggie

At ten-thirty that night, I stepped onto the deck of Sam's boat and knocked on her cabin door. I felt a little guilty about sneaking out of the house, but only a little. I was already in trouble.

I was surprised when it was opened by Reggie. Over his shoulder, I saw Sam sitting at the table. There was a big, hand-drawn map on brown wrapping paper taped on the wall over our lists. There was a big outline of the island on the paper.

When I sat down next to her, I saw Sam had showered, and I could smell shampoo and baby oil. I felt a little embarrassed about that because I'd changed into shorts and a t-shirt, but I didn't take a shower because I didn't think about it. I sniffed a little and thought I could still smell the dead boar. Then I had a thought: *Where was Reggie when Sam took a shower?* Then I remembered Sam didn't have a shower on the boat and she used the one in her mother's apartment. Then I felt like a jerk for thinking like that.

I sat down next to Sam, and she started talking. She used her pen to point at a blue line along the side of the paper. Then she drew a circle near the blue line. "This is where the bayou runs along through the golf course."

Reggie had a Red Stripe, the beer all the Jamaicans drink, open at the table. He nodded and took the pen. "Mangroves on each side of the bayou." He marked them with little squiggly lines along the canal line.

The trees and bushes are much different in Florida than they are in the north. I guess everything needs more water down here because it's so hot. Mangroves are these bushes that live next to salty water, and they look like regular bushes except they have all these roots under them. If you look at them from the water all you see is a forest of roots with some leaves on top.

"And here d' bridge." He drew a line where there was a bridge the golfers used to cross the bayou to get from one section of the course to the other. He moved his pen down the bayou and drew a couple of lines coming out from the bank and then some circles in the water of the bayou. "Dis is where d' Sheriff parks his boat." He tapped the lines against the shore. "And here is d' Manatee Hole."

Sam picked out a place called the Manatee Hole to hide Pinkie. It was this kind of round pool in the middle of the bayou near the golf course. Sailboats came in from the Gulf and moored there overnight, out of the wind.

Along with the plants and trees, there are some weird animals in Florida, too. The manatee is the weirdest. It sort of looks like a hippo with a big flipper where his back two legs should be. We've got a bunch of them in the canals around the island, but their favorite place is the Manatee Hole where they hang out all the time. It's a mammal so it needs to breathe, but for ten minutes or so, it hangs out on the bottom and then it comes to the surface with a big bubble, like somebody cut a big fart underwater, sticks its nose in the air, snorts, takes in a breath and goes back under. There are docks along the edge of the Hole where the tourists stand and watch them.

Reggie shifted and moved his pen to the top of the brown paper map. He tapped a spot where the public boat ramps were right before the bridge. "Now, Wendell Wolf, tomorrow night, you drop d' big pig here."

I nodded. I knew where it was. You drove past it every time you came over the bridge.

He pulled the map closer, pulled a bent pair of reading glasses out of his shorts pocket, and said, "OK, den. We be takin' d' big hog in my boat down the coast here," he ran his pen under the big bridge and down the coastline of the island a couple of miles. "Until we get to an opening of d' bayou, here." He put a little "x" on the map.

Sam had been quiet, but now she spoke up. "Won't someone see you?"

Reggie said, " 'Course, it be dark and Pinkie, d' big pig, she be covered in my boat."

We were quiet while that sunk in.

It was quiet in there for a while, and Reggie took a sip of his Red Stripe. Then he grinned. "OK, den." He burped.

All of a sudden I remembered something Reggie had said. "Who's *we*?"

Reggie smiled. "*We* be takin' d' big hog in d' boat 'cause I might need help." Reggie pointed his pen at me. "You and me, Wendell Wolf, you and me."

I started to say something. I was dropping Pinkie off at the public boat ramp with that idiot Jordan Minch. Why did Reggie expect me to go with him and Pinkie in the boat? But I shut up.

There was a silence and Reggie stood up. "OK, den. Get some sleep, kids. Big day t'morrow."

The boat rocked a little when he jumped off.

## Trouble Starts

Sam and I sat there and looked at each other. It was pretty late, about 11:30. Sam yawned, and then I yawned. I pulled a fresh sheet of graph paper out and taped it to the wall. I needed to make a list.

*Friday*:

1. Wendell checks out shell mound, figures out about burying Pinkie.
2. Wendell meets Jordan, picks up replacement boar, goes to shelter.
3. Wendell and Jordan meet T. Rex at shelter, exchange boar for Pinkie.
4. Wendell and Jordan meet Reggie at public boat ramp, 10 p.m.
5. Wendell, Reggie, and Jordan put Pinkie in Reggie's boat, go down bayou, hide Pinkie in Manatee Hole.

*Saturday:*

1. Bury Pinkie.

While we sat there and looked at the list, I realized that we'd thought all this stuff up without hearing from Nokoomis. I thought that was interesting, but I didn't say anything. Sam put her arm around my shoulders, and I'm glad I didn't say anything about that.

"Let's lie down on the bed a while."

It was like someone squeezed my chest. Really, I actually felt pressure in there and my breathing speeded up. I tried to be casual—like this wasn't the very first time in my lifetime that any girl suggested we lie down on her bed. "OK," I said, trying to sound interested but not trying to sound like I felt: *YES!*

I slid off the bench, and Sam followed me. She took my hand, but I didn't need to be led. Sam sat down on the bed first, and then she lay on her back. She looked at me, standing there, feeling like a dweeb, and patted the space next to her. She didn't say anything, she just smiled. I sat down and then I lay down, sort of on my side, facing her.

Before I could get settled, she gently grabbed my shoulders and guided me over on top of her. Sam was strong and big, and I kind of felt like I was being lifted, although I'm sure I helped out. On top of her that way, I could feel the various parts of her body up against mine. I wondered if I should move or something, but I stopped thinking when she kissed me. Then she slid her hands up under my t-shirt from behind, and I stopped thinking completely.

We kissed and kissed and I remembered the YouTube video and I think I was better than I was before. She smelled nice, a combination of shampoo, baby oil, and baby powder. Her skin was so smooth. At one point, when we stopped to get a breath (How often should you breathe when you're kissing? Mr. Sanders, any advice?), I flashed on Joel and the shitstorm that was going to happen the next morning when he got in his stinky Escalade. But then Sam kissed me again, and she pulled one hand out from under my shirt and slid it into the back pocket of my shorts. I don't know why, but that seemed so...personal. I forgot about Joel.

After a while we stopped kissing, and Sam started to breathe deeply. She murmured something just before she went to sleep. "You." I didn't hear her exactly because my ear was on the pillow. Anyway, I whispered, "I love you," back, just in case.

There's a *Hits of the 60's* CD my mother listens to in the kitchen. There's a song on there about this teenage boy and girl who go see a drive-in movie, and though they're not doing anything their parents wouldn't approve of (oh, sure they aren't), they fall asleep, wake up in the morning, and find themselves in *trouble deep.*

The boy wakes the girls up and, in a panic, asks her, "What are we gonna tell our friends when they say *'ooh la la!'*?"

A beam of sunlight coming through the boat's porthole woke me up. I sat up and we both found our phones at the same time. *7:23 a.m.* Sam almost squashed me as she rolled over me to get out of her little bed. "Shit. I've got a calculus test."

## I Face the Music and Sam Disappears

There were three messages on my phone, all from my mother:

**"Where are you?"**

**"I'm worried."**

**"Your father is very upset about his car, he was going to use it in the Heritage Day parade."**

Joel and my mom were working on the Escalade in our driveway, and they looked up as I walked across Granger's parking lot. It wasn't going to be easy to lie about where I'd been all night.

The Escalade had all of its doors open, my mom sprayed a deodorizer and Joel was in the front seat, blasting a leaf blower toward the back. That made me smile, which was stupid because it just made him madder. But, I'm sorry, the idea of Joel even knowing how to use the leaf blower and then using it on his car was funny.

Joel was dressed in golf clothes, and his shirt was already sweaty. He looked at me and said something right before he found the off/on switch on the blower. I was pretty sure I heard the word(s) "funk-up." (Mr. Sanders, is a hyphenated word single or plural?)

My mother put down her spray bottle and hugged me, but her nails cut into my shoulders. I think she was happy to see me, but she was pissed, too.

Then I took a sniff. The smell wasn't terrible. I forgot to take the crate of oranges out of the back and the smell was mainly fruity, but you could definitely tell something dead had been in there, that was for sure.

Then there was a crash because Joel unplugged the leaf blower and threw it against the house. The long blower nose thing broke off and a bunch of wires stuck out. Joel went over to the garage, jumped in his golf cart and laid rubber as he backed out of the driveway and drove away. When I saw the golf bag in the back, I remembered taking the money from the side compartment. After hearing him call me a "funk-up," I didn't feel so bad about that anymore.

With Joel headed down the street it was quiet, and my mother turned and walked toward the front door. "Get dressed. We have an appointment with Ms. Gordon at nine."

*Right. Should have seen this coming.*

It didn't go very well with Ms. Gordon. Usually she sees my side of the story, but "stealing" Joel's Escalade and sleeping over at Sam's in a 12-hour period was hard to explain. My mother asked Ms. Gordon if this was the beginning of my "adult anti-social impulse syndrome," which she read that kids who were adopted from Russia have.

I explained that Sam and I just fell asleep and it was all innocent (Kind of. I didn't tell them about the kissing.) But I couldn't explain why we took Joel's car. I just couldn't come up with a story. Without a good story about the Escalade, I didn't think either of them believed my story about Sam and me. And right in front of Ms. Gordon, my mother asked me if I knew about safe sex and whether she should buy me condoms. Right away I thought that was something a kid talked about with his dad, not his mom, but then I remembered my dad thought I was a funk-up, and besides that, it wasn't something you talked about in front of a guidance counselor.

Ms. Gordon just sat there, shaking her head. Every now and then, she lifted her glasses on the chain off her boobs and studied my file, as if she didn't already know every word. My mother asked Ms. Gordon if I should be confined to our house to "engage in a period of reflection," whatever that meant.

*My first reflection? I had a shitload of stuff to do: go get boar in Jordan's yard, steal Pinkie, put her in boat, take her down coast, help hide her, figure out how to bury her in a shell mound—all tonight. That was my reflection.*

But Ms. Gordon thought that was a "prudent course."

*OK, then.*

As my mother and I came back to the condo around 10 a.m., I saw Sam standing near the bait shop with her mother and some guy. I couldn't believe she didn't go to school after squishing me in the bed and being pissed about being late for her calculus test. Then I wondered about the guy. He was tall and dark like Sam. I knew right away. The guy was Bobby Dash. I didn't have a good feeling about this.

My mom and I stood in the kitchen, and she told me how disappointed she was in my behavior and that we would have a family conference later when my father got home. But I really didn't listen, I was too worried about Sam and that guy. I hurried to my room and checked out the window to see if Sam was still there. She wasn't.

I texted her;

**"Supp?"**

No response.

I looked back out the window. The parking lot over at Granger's was full of people and boats, but no Sam, her mother, or Bobby Dash.

For something to do, I pulled my list out of my pocket and studied it. It seemed like a lot, especially now when I had to sneak out of the house.

I texted Sam again:

**"Need to talk. Where r u????"**

Nothing. Shit. I sat and thought some more. I needed Sam. Who was that guy she was with? Was it really Bobby Dash? Why wasn't she in school? Did she hear me when I told her I loved her? How was she going to know I was supposed to stay in my house all day?

I went over and opened my door and heard my mother downstairs. It was Friday, and she was supposed to be at Banyan Bargains. *Was she staying home just to make sure I didn't go out? Shit.*

I checked my phone, but there wasn't any text.

I felt a little sick to my stomach. We had a big plan in place, I was supposed to stay in the house, and I couldn't reach Sam. My face felt hot. I sat down on my bed. I even thought I was going to cry.

Then a text came in from Sam:

**"Not burying Pinkie."**

I looked at it a couple of times, as this sunk in.

Not. Burying. Pinkie? It was pretty clear, but did she mean not "burying" as in "we're doing something else with her?"

I sent back a:

**"???"**

Right away, I got a response:

**"Stop everything."**

I looked at the message, and I saw red. I tried to concentrate. *Stop. Everything.* This time, there wasn't any doubt. "Stop everything" meant stop everything.

I couldn't believe it. We'd done so much. I'd been to the animal shelter and the frigging golf course. We'd recruited Reggie and that stupid Jordan Minch. T. Rex was set to meet me that night. There was a rotting boar under a tarp in Jordan's front yard. I stole that cash and his Escalade from Joel. I got caught and grounded. Plus, there was the kissing. As I thought about all of this, I got even more pissed.

Then I had a thought and texted:

**"WHAT ABOUT NOKOOMIS???"**

I had to wait a while until she responded:

**"No Nokoomis."**

I'm embarrassed to admit this, but I really did start to cry. I was more frustrated than sad, but some of my brain believed in Nokoomis. I mean, if she wasn't telling us what to do, who was? And, did this mean Sam and I would stop kissing? That made me even sadder.

So, I waited a while, sneaked out, and rode my bike back to the Inn. I needed to find Reggie. It was all I could think to do.

The Inn owns all these little cottages on the streets around it, and Reggie and the other yard guys are usually working somewhere in there. I found him blowing leaves on one of the little streets.

He turned off his blower as I rode up and looked to see if anyone was around. Then he smiled with his gold teeth and pushed his Rastacap back on his head. "Well, if it isn't Wendell Wolf. You find any 'dose wild boars, lately, Mon?" Then he laughed and laughed. I felt a little better. I figured Sam must have told him about the rotten pig in the Escalade. "Woo-ee. In d' Escalade, too, *woo-ee*." Then he laughed some more.

I waited for him to stop. I guess the whole story was funny, but I really wasn't in any mood to appreciate it. I looked around. Reggie was laughing so loud I wondered if anybody was going to come out of the cottages to see what was going on. I needed to talk to him about Sam.

A chirping noise stopped him, and he pulled his phone of his jeans pocket. He looked at the screen and his laughing face turned into a frown. "Dat girl. What be up wit dat girl, Wendell Wolf?"

I didn't read the message, but I had a feeling who "dat girl" was.

"Dat Sammy, she takes my boat, Mon. She takes my boat. Not good." He shook his head and handed me the phone.

I read the message from Sam:

**"Reggie, took your boat. Sorry."**

Reggie watched me read the message. "What you make of 'dat, Mon?"

I told him everything I knew, about Bobby Dash showing up, about the "No Nokoomis" and "Stop everything" messages.

Reggie stood there and listened. Every now and then he looked up and down the street. I finished the story, and he just stood there looking at me. Finally, after a couple of seconds, he said, "'Dis is a big problem, Mon. What you tink we should do?" He scratched his beard.

I nodded because I agreed, but I didn't say anything. I wanted Reggie to tell me what to do.

"What you gonna do?" He asked it again.

I just stood there and looked at him, and I didn't know what to say. I'd come to find him so he'd tell me what to do. "What do *you* think we should do?" I asked him the same question.

"Wendell Wolf, 'dis yo plan. You Sammy's boyfriend. Up to you, d' boyfriend." He paused and then he added, "And tell Sammy girl, Reggie needs his boat."

I thought about that. Reggie was older than I was and he'd known Sam a lot longer, but now I was the boyfriend and I had to decide this kind of shit? And besides, Sam and I were just kissing, did that make me her boyfriend? (I have to admit, I was proud about that boyfriend thing, though.)

Finally I thought of something. "If Sam has your boat, can you get another boat for tonight?"

Reggie thought about this a while, and then he nodded. "Work on it, Mon." He spat something into the street. "But tell Sammy she owes me, Mon." Then he flashed his gold teeth.

I felt my phone vibrate. I really hoped it was from Sam, but it was from my mom and I read the message once and then I read it again. And then I felt sick:

> **"Where are you? Your father and I are worried about your behavior with Sam Granger. Your father called Sheriff Pruitt."**

I couldn't believe it. Joel actually called Sheriff Pruitt? *Shit.* Then I looked around and pulled my bike behind a hedge. It was a small island, Sheriff Pruitt could be anywhere. And then I felt tears in my eyes. I couldn't believe they called the cops on me. They didn't understand I was just trying to help Sam. OK, we did take Joel's Escalade, but there wasn't any other choice. I stood there in the bushes until the mosquitos found me.

I didn't know where to go, so I went to Sam's boat. The Sheriff would have been there already.

I spread out on her bed, studied the wood planks in the ceiling, and looked around the room at her Calusa stuff on the walls.

I thought about the past week, Pinkie getting killed and what happened after that. I thought about Sam and how she was my only friend and she believed she was a Calusa and that her grandmother was a spirit in Pinkie. I thought about kissing Sam and I wondered if that's why I went along with her crazy plan to bury Pinkie. And then I thought about the trouble I was in. Taking Joel's car and stinking it up, falling asleep at Sam's. Stupid Joel calling the cops. And now Sam was missing in Reggie's boat and she wanted to call the whole thing off.

But somehow, I didn't want to stop. I mean, I suppose it would be easy to go home and apologize to everybody. I had the replacement pig over at Jordan's, but I supposed we could dump that in a canal somewhere. Some shark would love that.

There was music coming from somewhere nearby and I listened. I felt pretty alone. And stupid.

And then I thought of something really weird. Maybe I should ask Nokoomis what to do. How was I supposed to do that? Did Sam pray when she talked to Nokoomis? I never went to temple with Joel and my mom, so I really didn't know how to pray. Or maybe Sam just thought about Nokoomis really hard. Did she have some special words?

I stopped. Nokoomis was *Sam's* spirit grandmother. Did Nokoomis give guidance to other people? And then I worried about what Sam would think. Would it be OK with her if I talked to Nokoomis? I decided it would be OK.

I stared at a feather headdress on the wall. I felt a little lame. Pinkie was a dead pig, and what did Nokoomis look like? So I thought really hard about if Sam had a grandmother, what her grandmother would tell me to do (whatever she looked like). I breathed in and out because I thought I should do that, too.

I would like to tell you that Nokoomis spoke to me or that I got hit by a bolt of lightning, but what happened was, I woke up a couple of hours later.

I checked my phone—nothing from Sam, but a new message from my mom saying how disappointed she was in me. Just her, not Joel. Before I could stop myself, I sent her a message back:

> **"Won't be home tonight or tomorrow night. See you Sunday."**

And I pushed send. I sat there holding my phone wondering what I'd done. Then I stood up and brushed myself off and wondered why I did that. Maybe Nokoomis told me to.

I found some peanut butter and had dinner. I got out the list and studied it. I texted Reggie:

> **"Have another boat for tonight?"**

Right away, I got an answer;

> **"Yeah. Boat landing. 11 p.m."**

That was a relief.

I checked the list again. Shit. I was supposed to figure out how to dig in the shell mound. I hadn't done that yet. I checked the time. It was almost time to go over to Jordan's. I'd have to figure out the digging part on Saturday.

All of a sudden I heard police radio noises from the parking lot, and I looked out a porthole to see what it was. Sheriff Pruitt's SUV was parked by the bait shop, and he was standing there talking to Mandy

Granger. She was waving her big arms around (as usual) and yelling (as usual). I didn't hear what she said, but I figured it was about Sam being missing. And then I heard another voice off to the side—a woman's voice—and I moved my head to the edge of the porthole so I could see who it was. *Shit, Shit. Shit.* It was my mother. *Goddammit.* My mother and Sam's mother didn't even know each other. Sam's mom must have called the Sheriff too, and now they thought Sam and I were missing together. That thought put all sorts of images into my head. Would our pictures be on TV? Would they put out an amber alert?

Then, *shit*, the three of them turned and started walking toward the boat. I looked around. The cabin was so small, there really wasn't any place to hide. If I tried to get out the hatch door, they would see me. As quickly as I could, I crawled under the little booth table and scrunched into the corner. I grabbed Sam's soft blanket off a bench and I covered myself with it.

I heard steps on the deck and pounding on the hatch door. "Sam." It was a screech, so I knew it was her mom. She pounded again. "Sam, are you in there?"

Then there was a silence, and I heard her try the door. I held my breath. I felt someone stick their head in, and I heard heavy breathing. It must have been her mom. She stepped back. "See, she's not there."

I let my breath out because I thought they'd go away, but then I heard Sheriff Pruitt say, "Let me check."

Then I heard the hatch door open again, followed by a step on the stairs leading down into the cabin. I tried to shrink my body. Then the steps stopped. I smelled cigarettes. Then I saw my foot was sticking out just a little, and I slipped it back. There was quiet for about fifteen seconds. Then I heard Sheriff Pruitt whisper, "Be careful." Then the step, then the door. I breathed out. I couldn't believe that. Sheriff Pruitt was on our side?

I stayed still. Would my mom want to come down in the cabin, too? But there was quiet, and then I heard Sam's mom yelling as they walked away. At least I hoped they walked away. I stayed in my hiding place for maybe five minutes, until I couldn't stand it any longer. I needed to get to Jordan's, and my whole body was cramping. When I finally got out from under there, I checked the porthole. The Sheriff's

SUV was gone, and I couldn't see either my mom or Sam's mom. I thought about getting the list for another look, but I decided that was stupid. I was sure I could remember it all. And I needed to get going.

On the way, I thought about Sheriff Pruitt. He was a good guy.

## We Begin the Operation Without Sam

I slid off my bike at Jordan Minch's at exactly nine o'clock, just when it was getting dark. An old dog tied to the porch barked at me. Jordan sat in a pick-up truck in his driveway. When he saw me, he got out and held his hand down next to his leg. I just stood there until he spoke. "Give me the cash, dumb-ass."

I looked around. There wasn't anyone at his house or on the street, but he was acting like he was in *Breaking Bad*. It was stupid, but I pulled my wallet out of my shorts and found five twenties, folded them and stuck them in his hand. He looked at the money and grinned. He smelled like beer. "I never figured a punk like you."

That hurt my feelings, but instead of saying something, I said, "Let's do this." I figured that was something a drug dealer would say.

Jordan turned toward the pick-up, and I stopped him again. "What are you doing?"

He gave me his trademark smirk and spoke slowly like I was the idiot. "I'm going to back the pick-up truck up to the tarp over that rotten pig you dropped in my yard. Also, you owe me for a new tarp. That farting thing's ruined. Jesus, there's maggots all over it now."

I started to defend my replacement pig, but I stopped when I thought about how stupid that was. But if that wild boar had maggots on it, they came from Jordan's yard. Then I thought about maggots in the back of the Escalade. If that was true, no wonder Joel was so pissed. Stink was one thing, maggots was another.

I turned to him. "How are we going to lift the pig? I told you I needed to move a heavy load." I thought about how Sam and I needed the two Cubans' help in lifting the boar. I was sure Jordan and I couldn't do it, and I was pretty sure Pinkie was bigger than the boar.

Jordan just stood there looking dumb. I wondered if drug dealers had to do all the thinking for their people.

"Don't you have any equipment that will lift?" I wasn't thinking of anything specific, but frigging Jordan and his father, the tree kings of the island, must have something.

Jordan looked around the yard at all the equipment parked there. "Uh," he finally said, "Uh, the cherry picker." And he headed back into the yard. After a while I heard something start up, and then a bigger truck appeared. It was pretty dark and Jordan had the light on, so I had to wait until it got next to me to see what it was. I'd seen them all over, but I didn't know what they were called. It was a big truck with an arm on the back that lifted a little box in the air. A guy stood in the box and cut branches up in high trees. *That's a cherry picker? Sweet Jesus. We can't use that.* I almost started to cry in frustration. I mean, this was just the first thing on the list, and I had already frigged it up.

"What are we going to do with that, Jordan?"

Jordan swung out of the truck cab and into a seat next to the big mechanical arm. He started something up and moved some levers around. The little box thing lifted off the back of the truck into the air. "We can move it with this."

It sounded stupid to me.

Then Jordan got out of the truck. "Help me hitch up this leaf trailer." He grabbed the hitch on a little trailer, the kind the landscapers use for leaves and brush, and motioned for me to grab the other side. With Jordan guiding, we pulled it over in back of the cherry picker truck, and Jordan snapped something down that hitched it to the truck.

Then he stood up. "There." He seemed proud of himself. "Extra equipment costs extra." He held out his hand, this time, right out in the open. I pulled another twenty out of my wallet.

I checked my phone. It was already 9:30. We needed to load up the replacement pig up and go.

With the boar in the little trailer, we pulled up in the parking lot behind the Animal Shelter at 11:00. The lot was dark, and there was only one car there—hopefully T. Rex's—parked up against the building. The building was dark except for a light over the back door. It was a hot night, hot as the hottest summer day in Connecticut, and I was really sweating.

On the way over, Jordan did an OK job of steering the big truck, but he was terrible at shifting gears. The truck made horrible grinding noises every time he moved the gear lever, though I had to admit it was better than I could have done.

The rotten boar smell was awful when we first got it loaded, but when we got going the smell went out behind us so it wasn't so bad.

As the truck rumbled to a stop in the parking lot, the back door of the shelter opened. I could see T. Rex's silhouette in the light. Good. At least he was there.

Jordan got out and walked around shaking his head. I didn't tell him where we were going, because I figured he'd find some way to demand more money. "You're running drugs out of the effing Animal Shelter?" He did his smirk. "Cool, bro, very cool."

For a second I was proud to be complimented, until I remembered I wasn't actually a drug dealer, I was just stealing a frozen pig. Then I felt a little stupid.

T. Rex stepped out of the door and turned on a flashlight. He moved the beam back and forth over the cherry picker. "You're going to move it with that?"

I tried to sound confident, and I kept my voice down, "This kid is amazing with the picker, he does a great job."

The truth was, Jordan didn't know shit about running the cherry picker. I saw that back at his house.

"Right." T. Rex didn't sound convinced. "Well, the two of you come in here, I need help pushing the cart."

The three of us stood in front of the open freezer door. I waited for Jordan to say something stupid about all the frozen iguanas, but he was quiet, probably because it was so strange. Frozen Pinkie Pie was in the middle of the freezer. Somehow T. Rex had gotten her on this utility cart, the kind you see at a big hardware store to carry wood and stuff. Pinkie was just lying there on her side, not covered by a sheet, and she looked bigger than I remembered. I wondered if the cherry picker could pick her up.

With a lot of pushing and pulling, the three of us wheeled the cart outside. When we got to the door, Jordan complained that his hands were cold, that he was only doing the delivery and pick up and that I was going to owe him more money for loading. I just grunted OK, because I was busy with dead, cold, heavy Pinkie. Jordan was getting to be a pain in the ass.

Finally we got the cart out in the lot next to the trailer, and we stood there, breathing heavy. Jordan went over to the cab of the truck and came back with something in a paper bag that he started to drink from. I thought about saying something, but Jordan drinking beer out of a bag wasn't a big deal with everything I was doing that night.

I was still catching my breath, but I made a list in my mind. "OK, Jordan, first we need to lift the boar over and drop him on the ground next to the cart."

Jordan headed for the cherry picker controls, so I figured what I said was a good idea. I took a deep breath and held it and climbed in the trailer. Back at Jordan's, I hooked a chain around the boar (totally gross) and I left it in place after Jordan dropped it into the trailer. Now, I grabbed the same chain and yelled to Jordan. "OK, lower it down."

The cherry picker box came down so fast that I ducked, but then Jordan stopped it right before it squashed the boar. I heard him laugh, up there at the controls. *Dumb-ass.* I connected the chain and climbed down.

I yelled to Jordan, "OK, lift it up and put it beside the cart." Then I took a giant breath, which I hoped T. Rex didn't see because I was worried about what he'd say when he got a whiff of the rotting replacement boar.

There were cranking noises, and Jordan lifted the boar in the air. T. Rex started coughing and then gagging. "Holy shit, what's that stink?" He even bent over with his hands on his knees, which I thought was a little much. I mean, T. Rex cleaned up dog poop all day long.

I walked over to T. Rex and used my confident voice again. "This is our replacement pig. It's, uh, a little ripe, but I'm sure it will be OK."

Then, stupid Jordan lifted the cherry picker way too high and the boar started swinging around in circles. That was bad because it just whiffed the smell around every time it swung by.

T. Rex turned his flashlight on again and focused it on the spinning boar. Every time it swung by, its tusks flashed in the flashlight beam.

Finally Jordan dropped the boar too hard on the driveway next to the cart, it made a pretty bad "plop" when it landed, and the smell really got bad. Then everything was quiet. I saw T. Rex looking at me.

I ran over and unhooked the chain and pulled it out from under the boar. I was worried that T. Rex would stop this whole thing and make us take the boar back. Then I put the chain around Pinkie, and T. Rex stepped in to help. Together, we rolled and pushed her enough so she was hooked up to the cherry-picker box, and Jordan lifted her and dumped her in the leaf trailer, which sagged down a lot more than when it had the boar in it. Pinkie was a lot heavier than the skinny boar.

I kept looking at the time on my phone and every time I did, I checked for messages from Sam. There weren't any, and it was a lot later than I planned. I texted Reggie:

**"Going to be late. 1 a.m."**

We chucked the wild boar up onto the cart and pushed it into the shelter and the air conditioning inside made the boar...well, smell a little better.

But then things got worse when T. Rex saw the boar in the bright lights. "F#$k no, Mop Midget, this ain't gonna work."

My heart sank. "Why?"

"This f#$king boar doesn't look anything like your girlfriend's pig. It's skinny and it's hairy, plus it has tusks. And it's brown. Your pig was pink. F#$king Hultz will see the difference right off."

Luckily, Jordan decided he didn't want to be in on this, and he said he was going to stay outside with the "brewskis."

I stood there and just looked at T. Rex. For the second time that night, I thought I was going to cry. Finally, I got it together so I could speak.

"Look, T., I told you, this is for my *girlfriend*." I looked at him for a reaction, but I didn't see one. Then I thought of something else that would make a difference to him. *Officer Hultz, he hated her.* "And, uh, Officer Hultz shouldn't have shot Pinkie. She really doesn't like animals."

T. Rex thought about this as he walked around the cart looking at the dead wild boar. "I don't know, man, I don't know. There's no f#$king way this is going to fool Hultz."

I spoke up. "I thought you said she doesn't come to all the cremations."

He nodded. "That's true, man. If she's not here, all I need is a body. But it's got to look something like your pig."

I pleaded with him some more. "Isn't there anything we can do?" I checked my phone for the time. *Shit.*

I watched him rub his hand along the hair on the boar's side like he was looking for something. Finally he stood up. "OK. Two things. First, I need you to keep Hultz away from here at two tomorrow afternoon. We can't take the chance of having her here."

I thought fast. "Yeah, I can do that."

"OK, that's the easy part. Now there's the second thing."

If this were a fairy tale, I would tell you that cutting the hair off a dead, stinking wild boar was simple. But it's not a fairy tale, this really happened, and it was awful.

T. Rex left and came back with some clippers, the kind barbers use, some shaving cream, and a bunch of razors. When I asked him about the razors, he told me the vets used them to shave dogs and cats before they were "fixed." That made me feel a little better. If a vet could shave an animal, I guessed I could.

He handed me a plastic bucket of hot water and a sponge. "You start at the butt, I'll start at the head, use the clippers first, then sponge on some water, rub in some shaving cream, wait a bit and shave her down. You know the drill."

Well, the truth was, I didn't know the drill. I didn't shave. I mean, I ran a razor over my face a couple of times, but I really didn't need to. My first actual shave was this dead boar. And even if vets shaved cats and dogs, I thought doing it to a boar was a lot harder.

It took an hour. I had to go outside and tell Jordan and pay him some more money. I texted Reggie and told him we were going to be even later. I clipped when T. Rex told me to and I shaved when T. Rex told me to. And boars don't have regular hair, either, they have bristles. We used maybe twenty razors. I got a rash on my arm from pig bristles. The whole thing was totally gross.

When we were done, we had a really ugly, pink (but not as pink as Pinkie), hairless replacement pig. It was skinnier than Pinkie, but it might work.

T. Rex even got some pliers and pulled the tusks out of its mouth.

It was disgusting, but I agreed with him—everyone would know that pet pigs don't have tusks. He tried to give them to me, but I didn't want them. Finally, at midnight, we wheeled the cart with our shaved replacement pig into the freezer and covered it with a sheet.

I stood at the back door and thanked T. Rex. It was still hot as hell outside, and both of us were sweaty again. I was covered with stinky, soapy boar bristles. Jordan sat in the cab of the cherry-picker drinking beer, and Pinkie Pie, covered by a tarp, was in the leaf trailer.

Then T. Rex stuck his hand out for a real handshake. "That girlfriend of yours must be something, Bro. She's lucky to have you."

That reminded me that Sam was missing, although I didn't really forget it, it just went to the back of my brain.

I let go of his hand and said, "Yeah, she is."

Then I wondered about whether Sam was lucky to have me. I thought about everything I was doing, and I added, "And yeah, I guess she is."

## Moving a Frozen Pig

When we pulled out of the shelter parking lot onto the highway, the first thing I did was text Sam again. No response. I guess I didn't expect any, but it made me feel lonely. Of course, there was Jordan and everything seemed OK with him except for the fact that his six-pack of Budweiser was now a one-pack. Jordan had beer number five in one hand, he had his headphones on, I could hear heavy metal, and he keep pounding the beat on the steering wheel. I turned and looked behind us and saw the little trailer with the big mound of tarp-covered Pinkie Pie, I was at least happy about that.

I texted Reggie and told him we were on our way.

Then there was this really loud bang and a screeching noise from behind us. "Holy shit," Jordan yelled, and he dropped his beer on the floor. The truck jerked back and forth. I looked back and saw flames coming from both sides of the trailer. It was swerving around like a hooked fish on a line.

Jordan jerked the wheel, and we sort of went off the road. Then he pulled into this gravel lot and slid to a stop.

One of the tires on the trailer was gone. It just fell off and rolled somewhere. The bottom of the trailer had torn gouges in the road, and that's what caused the flames. I guess we were lucky the trailer (and Pinkie) didn't catch on fire, but standing there in the middle of the night with a ruined trailer and a frozen pig, I didn't feel especially lucky. Jordan let loose a huge beer burp behind me, and then he said, "Shit, man, wrecking the trailer's going to cost you more."

"Frog you, Jordan. Just shut up." I know I shouldn't have said it. I mean, Jordan was my only way of getting Pinkie to Reggie's boat, but I couldn't help it. I was tired of his shit. What kind of trailer loses a wheel?

Jordan just stood there. I felt bad and I also knew I needed his help, so I apologized. "Sorry. I'm under a lot of pressure."

He burped again. "No problem, Dude."

I was no expert, but just to be sure, I asked, "We can't use the trailer anymore, right?"

Jordan laughed, "No way, Dude."

I almost told him to stop calling me Dude, but I caught myself.

Right away I thought of giving up, just calling my mom and Joel, tell them where I was and take whatever shit they'd give me, but then I thought of Sam and what she'd want me to do. True, she was missing, but she was my friend, and Pinkie deserved to be buried. So I tried to think.

"Jordan, can you drive the truck with the cherry picker up in the air?"

I heard a sucking slurping noise and the crush of a beer can behind me. "Dude, you aren't supposed to do that."

There was a silence and I asked, "Have *you* ever done it?" I mean, it seemed obvious. Of course he'd done it.

"Uh, yeah. A couple of times."

That's all I needed to hear. "OK, unhook the trailer and bring the cherry picker down close over Pinkie. I'll get the chains around her."

Ten minutes later, Pinkie swung back and forth from the bottom of the picker, maybe twenty feet above and behind the truck. The trailer was unhooked and beside the road.

Jordan came back to look. He had what I assumed was beer #6 in his hand. Pinkie swung slowly around in a circle. Jordan shook his head. "I don't know, man. I mean, don't you think people will wonder?"

After we dropped the trailer, the ride didn't get any easier. Pinkie swung around from the cherry picker and the truck wobbled and veered from side to side. Jordan even told me to hold his beer because he needed to drive with both hands. I thought about taking a sip because I was real thirsty, but I hated the beer smell and Jordan's spit was in there. So I stayed thirsty.

When we pulled into the boat landing parking lot, it was 2:15 in the morning. There were cars and trailers parked in the lot—night fishermen, I guessed—but there wasn't anyone in the booth out front where you paid your money. That was a relief. I was worried about that because they might ask about the swinging tarp-bundle in the back. Plus, I didn't have any parking money. I forgot to put it on my list. Bad planning.

I told Jordan to drive down to the docks and stop and turn the truck off so I could find Reggie. I got out and started down to the row of docks. There were streetlights down there, so I could see pretty well. Then, *fudge!* I saw it. The Sheriff's boat was at the second dock in the row. And *double fudge!* It was on. I mean, it was running. I could hear it making a low bubbling noise from the back. *I was caught. How did Pruitt know?*

I didn't see anyone on the boat, so I just kept walking. I thought about running away, but that seemed like a bad strategy. I got right next to the boat and started to walk by, when someone stood up from the shadows behind the steering wheel. "Wendell Wolf, is dat you, Mon?"

I almost pissed my pants and maybe worse, but then I recognized the voice and the accent. Reggie. *Whew.* Then, *Reggie was in the Sheriff's boat? How'd that happen? Sweet Jesus, were we going to get in trouble. Nokoomis, if you're there, protect us from Sheriff Pruitt.*

I heard the clunk as a beer bottle was thrown in a bucket, and I knew it was a Red Stripe. Then this figure in a Rastacap stepped into the light. "Wendell Wolf, it's about time, Mon, let's get dis ting goin'. Where's dat cold pig?"

I thought about asking Reggie how he came to be in the Sheriff's boat, but I figured that could wait. We needed to move fast.

But then Reggie started to laugh. It started as a giggle and then it became a laugh and then his whole body shook. He bent over with his hands on his knees.

At first I didn't know what was happening, but then he caught his breath and stood up and pointed and started laughing again.

It was Pinkie. Reggie saw Pinkie swinging around under the cherry picker box.

At first, I didn't think it was funny, after everything I went through to get there. But then I started to laugh along with Reggie. I didn't think it was as funny as he did, but I guess it did look bizarre.

Finally, we both stopped laughing and I stood in back of the truck and directed while Jordan backed the truck up so Pinkie was right over the boat.

Jordan stopped, and he got out and came around back to see where we were. "Dude, the Sheriff's boat? Cool. You guys have got some serious balls." He paused and looked at the boat, then at Reggie. "I'm going to need some more dough. This deal's got a higher risk factor than I thought."

I thought about yelling at him again, but we were almost there. Pinkie hovered right over the boat, swinging in a circle. "Fine, Jordan. You know I'm good for it. Let's just get this done." He thought about this, nodded, crushed his beer can, stuck it in a trashcan, and went back to the controls.

"OK, Mon," Reggie yelled, "Set her down easy." Jordan did a pretty good job of moving Pinkie with the cherry picker and lowering her onto the deck at the rear of the boat. I crawled in and undid the chains. The Sheriff's boat was a lot bigger than Reggie's, which was good because Pinkie's 350 lbs. squashed the rear of the boat down in the water and lifted the bow way up high.

All of a sudden I heard a clunk on the dock. When I looked over, I saw a fishing boat, the ones the fishing guides use with this kind of tower on top. It pulled up a couple of docks away. It used one of those little electric motors—which is why we didn't hear it come up.

"Hey, Sheriff, what's going on?"

Reggie and I stood frozen-still.

There was a moment or two of silence. Then I figured I better say something. I got my deepest voice ready. "Just finishing up an investigation here. Nothing to see." I hoped that would get them to leave us alone.

Then Jordan jumped out of the truck and blundered in. "It's a drug deal. We're picking up evidence." I couldn't believe it. Why would he tell them that? *What a dick.*

"Oh, yeah? Let me take a look." I saw one of the guys hop out of his boat and head toward us.

All of a sudden Reggie stepped out from behind the steering wheel. He had taken off his Rastacap and his dreadlocks went all over the place. Then he hit the guy in the face with a powerful flashlight beam. "Stay where you are, Mon. Dese boys and I are undercover. We can't be havin' you men see our faces."

The guy stopped. Actually, he had to stop because he was blinded by the light. (Song title, check it out) "OK, OK." He raised his hands up over his face. The Sheriff's flashlight that Reggie used was as powerful as a laser.

"Just move d' boat away from d' dock and float away. We be done here soon." I didn't know Reggie was great at giving orders.

The guys got back in their boat and pushed off. Just before their motor started I heard, "Pruitt's got Bob Marley workin' undercover." And then laughter.

We stood there until they went away, and then Reggie said, "OK, Wendell Wolf. You and me, we goin' for a ride."

He called out to Jordan. "And you, Mr. Talkie-Talkie, can you get this truck back on d' island in one piece, or should you stay here for a while and sleep it off?"

Jordan sounded hurt. "Hey, Dude, I was just tryin' to help." There was a cranking noise as he lifted the cherry picker.

Reggie fired up the engine on the Sheriff's boat. It sounded huge. I thought about yelling "thank you" to Jordan but we were moving, he was getting in the truck, and probably drug dealers didn't thank each other after a deal.

We pulled away from the ramp at the public boat landing, and when we got away from the streetlights at the dock I realized how bright the moon was. Then I remembered that the next night was the full moon. Bury Pinkie on the night of the next full moon in sacred ground. That was why I was there.

I checked my phone:

**"Your father and I hope you're all right."**

**"Going to bed now, worried."**

I felt bad about that, but what could I do?

Reggie pointed to a cooler. "Yoo-hoo in der, Mon." For just a second, I thought Sam was back. She packed Yoo-hoo for me. But then I realized that was stupid, and Reggie probably saw me drinking it in Sam's cabin. Anyway, it was nice of Reggie to remember. I thanked him, got a can, and almost drank it in one swallow, I was so thirsty. It was so hot, and I guess moving a frozen pig with that finking Jordan

Minch made me nervous so I sweated even more. I knew this because when I sat down next to Reggie on this high bench behind the steering wheel of the Sheriff's boat, he said, "You really got d' stink on, Mon. I know dat's not Pinkie, because ole Pinkie still be frozen."

I started to explain, but I looked at him in the dark with his face lit up by this little light over the boat's dashboard, and I could see his gold teeth so I knew he was smiling.

Reggie wore a pair of old shorts and sandals and a Chicago Bulls jersey. We were cruising just off the beach, going pretty slow so we wouldn't attract attention. I told him about my night with Jordan and T. Rex and the animal shelter and the cherry picker, and after he got done laughing his ass off again, he told me about "borrowing" the Sheriff's boat. According to Reggie, the Sheriff never used the boat at night unless there was an emergency or he was trying to catch dope smugglers. I didn't ask him how he knew the Sheriff wasn't going to be catching dopers that night, and I just hoped he wouldn't get a call in the middle of the night and run down to the dock and find his boat gone. According to Reggie, everybody knew the Sheriff kept the keys to the boat on a hook in a shed at his dock, and everybody knew where he hid the keys to the shed, too. It's a small island.

So there we were, with the motor bubbling along and the bow of the boat up in the air with a 350 lb. weight in the back. I had another Yoo-hoo, and I crawled over the Pinkie mound and peed off the back of the boat. Every couple minutes I checked my phone for a message from Sam, because I had my ringer off. Nothing. Even with everything I was doing that night, I felt sad and worried without her. She should be there.

"Where do you think Sam went?" I just threw the question out there. I really didn't think Reggie knew, but I wanted to talk about Sam. I also didn't know if Reggie would talk about Sam. They were friends, and sometimes friends don't talk about each other. Anyway, my question was met by silence.

Finally, he answered. "Don't know, Mon, but she in my boat."

Well, at least he answered.

"How long have you known Sam?"

"Since she a baby, Mon."

I kept quiet.

"Sam's momma, Mandy? She a good girl, but she drinks too much and likes to smoke her weed."

I nodded, like I wanted him to know I was listening, but that was wasted, because it was dark and I was in the back of the boat with Pinkie so he couldn't see me. But he kept talking.

"I just come here from Jamaica. Mandy, she be pregnant wit' Sam. Big as a house, she was. Everybody say, Sam's daddy be 'dat Bobby Dash. I mean, I don't know, dat's what people say. Sam's momma, she be wit lots of guys."

"So you were Sam's friend, growing up?" I heard the cap twist off a Red Stripe and clink into a bucket.

"Yeah, friend, yeah. She always around marina. Everybody be her friend. 'Course she be takin' care of her momma, soberin' her up and such."

"How old was she then?"

"Mebbe, she start when she five or six, puttin' out her momma's cigarettes when she come home drunk, goin' to get her in bars, dat sorta ting. We all feel bad fo' Sam, puttin' up wit dat shit." He was quiet for a while and I heard slurping noises. " 'Course we all got shit goin' on in our lives."

"When did she start thinking she was a Calusa?"

"Oh, dat started when she twelve or thirteen, I remember cause it when she filled out. Woo-ee, Mon."

I felt jealous, I knew that was stupid and at least I didn't say anything.

"She found dat picture in her momma's drawer, and she went to town. Got all dat Calusa stuff, d' feathers and such. Read all dose books. Dat Sammy, she one smart girl, always readin'. Dat's when she got Pinkie Pie. I mean people around here, dey droppin' animals off at Granger's all d' time, but a pig? Where did a pig come from on 'dis island? Anyway, dat pig and Sam, dey become best friends."

Reggie was quiet for a while. There were some houses nearby, and when he started talking again, his voice was lower.

"D' spirit animal ting, dat was a surprise. I mean, all d' folks from d' islands here, we familiar wit Voodoo and such, so spirit animal? We say OK! But Sam talk to dat pig all d' time, unusual for white girl. So, d' Calusa 'ting? It make sense to us, do you see?"

I saw him turn back to look at me, and I nodded. Not because I understood, because it all seemed pretty weird to me, but because Reggie wanted me to understand.

Then he changed subjects. "What you really want to know is, if Sammy-girl likes you. All deese questions, right?"

Whoa! This was a total change in the subject. I didn't say anything while I thought about it. Yeah, he had a good point, that's where I was headed. But I didn't plan it out. I think.

"Uh, yeah."

"OK, knew it. Can't tell you dat, Mon. Certainly, you d' only boy I ever seen her sweet on, course I don't know why, Mon...."

He turned back toward me from the steering wheel. I could see he had a big grin. "Just joshin' you, Mon. You need another Yoo-hoo?"

I shook my head.

He turned his back to me so he could keep driving. "Sammy has a hard life, her momma a mess and all dat workin' at d' marina."

Then he turned the engine off and we drifted.

He turned and faced me, and I could see his face in the moonlight. "You good for her, Mon. She never had no friends."

I nodded.

"But, Wendell Wolf, don't hurt Sammy, you hear?"

I nodded, but I felt tears in my eyes. I was turning into such a titty-baby.

"Your people, dey live here year-round but dey winter people, right? But Sammy, she an islander. And boys your age, dey usually interested in one ting, you know what I be sayin'?"

I was quiet. I knew exactly what he was saying, but I didn't want to admit it.

"You and your people, Mon, you can leave any time. But, Sammy, she have a hard time leavin' what wid all she do for her family and such at d' marina. You know what Reggie is sayin'?"

I nodded again. Reggie watched me carefully. I don't know why, but what Reggie said made me like Sam even more.

Reggie was quiet for a while and I waited for him to say something. But instead, he changed the subject. "Oh yeah, d' Manatee Hole.

Sammy-girl, she'll like dat place. Good place, too."

I breathed out, and I could swallow again.

As I said, I didn't know anything about getting around in a boat, but I think we went partway down the island in the bay, then turned into the bayou and went along there for while, and I could see the mangroves on either side of us. Reggie had the lights on in the front and back of the boat, and he even had the police radio turned on low. So I guess if anyone saw us, it looked like we were on patrol. That made me feel good, until I remembered if a call came over the radio and the Sheriff needed his boat, we were screwed. That made me sweat even more in the hot night.

I felt the boat turn, and we headed into a little canal I could barely see in the moonlight. Reggie whispered, "Secret passageway, Mon. No one see us here." I wondered if it was one of the routes Reggie and his buddies used to bring in dope.

I knew we were near the Manatee Hole, because I could see the lights on the radio tower in the middle of town. All of a sudden, mangroves brushed up against the sides of the boat. The canal was getting narrower. Reggie turned the motor off, and I could hear a whirring noise from back there. When I looked around, I saw the motor was out of the water. Reggie jumped out from behind the steering wheel and grabbed this really long pole that was in a holder along the deck. He headed to the back of the boat with the pole. Right then, I felt the boat hit something underneath, and we stopped.

"Shit, Mon. We missed d' tide. I knew we was too late." That was Reggie from the back. I didn't exactly know what he meant but I knew it wasn't good news.

Reggie pushed on the pole, but we didn't move. Then he jumped down in the water and pushed. Then he told me to get in the water and pull a rope on the front. I did it, but it scared the shit out of me. There are all sorts of things in the water in Florida. Anyway, I got in, and the water only went up to my knees. And my knees are closer to the ground than most people's. It was really shallow. No wonder we were stuck.

We got back in the boat. All of a sudden we were covered with mosquitos. Reggie found some bug spray under the seat, and we sprayed ourselves with it, but they still buzzed around looking for a place to bite. Reggie pulled a Red Stripe out of the cooler and popped the top. He went to the back of the boat and peed over the side.

"What are we going to do now?" I felt stupid asking it, but I couldn't just sit there in the dark mangrove swamp swatting bugs. I looked at my phone. It was 3:33 a.m.

I think I heard Reggie sigh. "We wait, Mon. D' tide gone out. Tree hours she be back in, den we move."

"Three hours?" I sounded like I was whining, but I was just repeating what he said while I tried to remember what time the sun came up.

"Yeah, Mon. If you be at d' landing on time, d' tide be right. But now we stuck fo' tree hours."

I wanted to tell him why we were late, but I already did that, so it didn't make any difference. I tried to think. In three hours the sun would be coming up. Fishing guides picked up customers on those docks at the Manatee Hole. I wondered how early that happened. I looked at my phone again. No message from Sam. I slapped a mosquito on my forehead, and I heard snoring from the back of the boat. Reggie had his Rastacap over his eyes, and he used a life vest as a pillow. He was sound asleep. I had too many Yoo-hoos that night to sleep, so I just sat there and looked at the stars. After a while I made a list, and I felt better. Then I sent a text to Sam.

## I Miss Sam and Write a List of What We Need To Do

It wasn't my idea to put this next text to Sam in this book. Mr. Sanders said it had to be in there to show the "depth of my character," whatever that means. It's a little embarrassing, but it's not the only thing that was embarrassing. Remember, I shaved a dead boar!

**"Dear Sam, Where r u? Here in Sheriff's boat (don't ask) w Reggie. It's 5 am and we r stuck on bottom in a secret canal and have to wait til tide comes in. Wish u were here, but u probably needed to go somewhere. Sorry about Bobby Dash and sorry u r sad. I'm following our plan (making some changes) so Pinkie gets buried tonight. I think I talked to Nokoomis. I know u must be smiling. Anyway—question. Have we been kissing so I'll help you with Nokoomis or did u really feel like kissing? I know that sounds stupid, but I've been sitting out here all night and I've been thinking about that (along with listening to Reggie snore and killing mosquitos and worrying about something big bumping against the side of the boat) Sorry about the kissing question. I like you no matter what. Anyway, I wish u were here. Even if u aren't, I'll bury Pinkie. Wendell.**

**P.S. Sending u my latest list in case u get back and want to help.**

**P.P.S. I think I love you.**

1. **Get Sheriff's boat floating again.**
2. **Hide Pinkie in Manatee Hole.**
3. **Breakfast.**
4. **Help Reggie take Sheriff's boat back.**

5. 2 pm—Do something to keep Officer Hultz away from shelter.
6. Figure out how we dig hole under Big Banyan.
7. Figure out how to get Pinkie from hiding place to Big Banyan.
8. Funeral? Find out about Calusa funerals for spirit animals.

## Our Big Day

**6:30 a.m.**

I felt the boat lift off the sand just when the sun came up. I checked my phone and there wasn't a message from Sam. It was 6:30 a.m., just like Reggie said it would be when the tide came in. I smelled awful—leftover dead boar stink with some shaving cream mixed in and two days of sweat on my t-shirt mixed with bug spray. Around 5 a.m., I'd figured out that there are little bugs you can't see that bite you under your shorts. I sprayed everywhere.

Reggie rolled over and got up. The first thing he did was pee off the back of the boat. I heard a bottle open and a slurp. His first Red Stripe of the day. He picked up the long pole, stuck it in the water, and started to push. And we started to move. I got a Yoo-Hoo out of the cooler. We were on the move.

Right away I figured out riding around in the Sheriff's boat was more dangerous in the daylight than in the dark, even though we were in this tiny canal with high mangroves brushing up against us.

In the distance, I heard a sound in the air and I knew it was a helicopter, but that wasn't unusual. Helicopters flew over the island all the time. But this one was lower and louder, and it was early. Rich people who live on an island don't like to hear helicopters early in the morning. This one must have been special.

All of a sudden, Reggie threw his pole down and jumped into the water.

"Wendell Wolf, get in d' water, Mon. Help me push d' boat in here." I put my phone down and jumped into water up to my chest. The bow of the boat was high over my head, but I grabbed the rope in the front.

"Pull d' boat into d' opening dere."

There was a dent in the mangroves along the canal about the size of a little driveway. It didn't look like the boat would fit in there, but Reggie pushed and I pulled and I got smashed into a bunch of mangroves in front, but the boat just fit. The mangroves on either side kind of folded over the decks.

Right then, the helicopter flew over fast. It said "Sheriff's Department" on the side.

"Wendell Wolf, help me pull Pinkie off d' deck."

I hesitated. "Get back here, Mon. Now!"

I pushed through the mangroves to the back of the boat. Reggie had hold of the ropes on one side of the tarp covering Pinkie. I grabbed the ropes on the other side, and we pulled. At first nothing happened to Pinkie, but the boat moved backwards. "Shit, Mon." Reggie grunted and then pulled harder on the rope and lifted his legs out of the water and braced them on the back, next to the motor. Then we pulled again.

Pinkie came off the deck and hit the water like someone dropped a big boulder off a bridge. The tarp flipped up in the air and landed on Reggie and me. There was a huge low noise that's hard to describe when you write it. "Fa-voomp" is the best I can do. Pinkie splashed when she hit the water and splashed again when she came bobbing back up.

After we pulled the tarp off our heads, Reggie and I stood there in the water, steadying Pinkie. Reggie untied one of the tarp ropes and wrapped it around Pinkie's neck. Did you know a frozen pig could float? Maybe we covered that in Science class, but I don't think so. Anyway, Pinkie floated.

Pinkie was still cold, which actually felt kind of good because the air was already getting hot. Off in the distance we heard the helicopter buzzing along, but it didn't sound like it was coming toward us.

"What are we going to do?" I looked at Reggie. It was his idea to jump in the water. Maybe he had the next idea.

"Any your stuff in d' boat?"

I thought a second or two. "My cellphone. Why?"

"Go get it, 'den. Time to say goodbye to d' Sheriff's boat." He let go of Pinkie, cupped his hands, and gave me a boost up into the boat. I found the phone on the deck and looked to see if there was a message from Sam. There wasn't.

I eased myself off the back of the boat with my phone in my hand above my head.

Reggie had already pulled Pinkie back into the canal from our hiding place. He was up to his waist in water. That meant it would be up to my neck. I waded out to him.

He took off his Rastacap. "Put d' phone in 'dere."

I hesitated. Reggie kept his dreadlocks in that hat. They didn't look very clean to me, but I didn't really know. Why did he want my phone in there?

Reggie interrupted whatever I was going to think next. "Just do it, Wendell Wolf. Reggie be tired of 'dis."

I dumped the phone in, and he stuck the Rastacap on his head.

"Now, we needs to drag 'dis pig down d' canal to d' Manatee Hole, and d' Sheriff, he be lookin' for us."

I felt something curl against my leg. It happened once and I didn't say anything. Then it happened again and I jumped. *Was it a snake or just seaweed? Some Florida asshats let their pets go, and they became monsters in the Everglades. We weren't far from the Everglades. Was it a python? Did pythons bite or did they squeeze you to death?*

I danced up and down a little, trying to keep my feet off the bottom. Maybe Reggie was pissed at me, but I couldn't stand it any longer. "Something's hitting me on the leg." I said it to Reggie's back because he was in front, pulling on the rope and I was in back, pushing on her big frozen butt.

Then it happened again. I jumped again. It was definitely alive.

Reggie just grunted.

It was hard work pulling Pinkie along in the water, and it was getting really hot. I was pushing, but Reggie was doing most of the work, pulling Pinkie along. Other than his grunt, he didn't answer.

I tried again. I tried to sound casual. "Yeah, I felt it again. Any snakes in here?"

There was a silence as we took a couple of steps more, and then he answered. "Yeah Mon, but d' ting hittin' your leg likely be a small shark."

*Sweet Jesus!* That made me dance again. People caught sharks all over the island. Kids from the high school stayed out on the beach all night fishing for sharks with chunks of bait on huge hooks. The world record hammerhead shark was caught just off the island three years ago. And the thing hitting my leg was a shark?

I tried to keep my voice low because I didn't want to sound scared. "Uh, how small?" Then, when he didn't answer right away, "Do they bite?"

We were in deeper water now, up to my shoulders. I thought we must be getting near the Manatee Hole, but with the mangroves on either side of us like a wall, I still didn't know where we were.

"Prob-ly no, Mon. Unless your leg smell like fish." And then he laughed and that made me feel a little better. But then I remembered my leg smelled like shaving cream and boar. *Would that be a problem?*

Then Reggie stopped, and we held floating Pinkie between us. I wanted to get my phone out from under Reggie's cap and check to see if there was a message from Sam, but I didn't because now there was a current in the water and I had to keep hold of Pinkie's tail.

Reggie turned back toward me and whispered, "OK, Mon. Around d' corner is d' Manatee Hole. Need to figure out where to hide d' pig."

Reggie let go of Pinkie's ear, and I braced my legs because I had to hold her against the current. Reggie waded forward to where it looked like our little canal ended, but it was actually just a sharp turn into the bayou. I saw him peek around the corner and come back.

"OK, Mon. Just as I 'tout. Dere's an open mooring buoy. You tie Pink up dere."

I thought for a second or two. I had been up all night, and I was tired, and I was hungry. And I was standing in shoulder-deep water with what might be man-eating sharks. "How?"

Reggie got close to me so he whispered right in my ear. "Dere's people on d' boats out dere. We be very quiet, Mon." Then he held onto my shoulder and stuck Pinkie's rope into my hand. "You need to swim out dere and pull d' pig and tie dis rope on d' mooring ball."

"*I* have to swim? Why don't we do it together?"

Of course, I could swim. Every kid in my Connecticut town took swimming lessons. But I wasn't a great swimmer. I wasn't great at anything athletic.

But then Reggie said, "I can't swim, Mon." I looked at him, but he looked away. I mean, Reggie was a Jamaican. Jamaica is an island surrounded by the ocean. Aren't all Jamaicans really good swimmers? I know, another stereotype.

He shrugged his shoulders. "OK, Mon. When you swim, you keep Pinkie 'tween you and d' other boats. If dey look, dey tink it's a big manatee."

I wanted to argue, but we needed to get this done. I waded down to the corner of our little canal and took a look. There were three sailboats moored in the cove, and the open mooring buoy was between us and them. I didn't see anyone on the sailboats. It was still early Saturday morning. On the other side of the Manatee Hole was the line of docks where people stood and watched the manatees and the dolphins. There were a couple of people out there drinking coffee.

I guessed I could do it, but I wanted to ask Reggie one more time.

I waded back to him.

When I got near, he whispered, "What you tink, Wendell Wolf? Can you do 'dis for Sammy-girl?"

I was going to ask him why he couldn't swim, but when he mentioned Sam, I stopped. Instead, I looked at Pinkie. All you could really see was her pink back humped out of the water. I supposed she looked a little like a manatee.

"OK, I'll do it."

We pushed and pulled Pinkie to the end of the canal and stopped at the turn. I took off my t-shirt, but I left my sneakers on. If a shark was going to bite me, it was going to get a mouthful of sneaker first. I got down in the water to see if people could see me behind Pinkie's back sticking out of the water. Reggie said he couldn't see me, but he probably would lie just to get me to do it.

I pushed off, and right away the water was over my head. I know because I tried to touch the bottom with one foot even though I was still scared of snakes and sharks down there. I did a kind of a frog-kick as I pushed Pinkie ahead of me. I tried to keep my head really low in the water, but I still needed to breathe.

I did a lot better than I thought I would. There was a pretty good current with the tide coming in, and I got Pinkie out to the buoy, no problem, other than being scared shitless that some shark would be cruising along and decide it wanted a nice, frozen ham breakfast. I tied her up, and then I realized I had to swim back and couldn't hide my head behind Pinkie. So I swam the whole way back underwater with my eyes open just in case I'd see a shark, in which case, I'd set a world bayou speed record. When I got back to the canal, I lifted my head and saw Reggie sneaking his head around the corner of the mangroves watching.

I stood up, and Reggie patted me on the shoulder. I was still breathing hard from the swim, but I felt good. Together, we stuck our heads out to see how Pinkie looked.

She floated out there with her back out of the water, and she did look like a manatee except for one thing. "She's still pink," I whispered, which was kind of true, but being frozen made her kind of gray, too.

Reggie patted me on the shoulder and stuck the cap and phone back on my head. "Albino manatee, Mon. Rare. Let's get out of here. Sammy-girl be proud of you."

**7:00 a.m.**

Cutting through some backyards and over some fences that Reggie knew about, we made it back to the marina. Reggie needed to get to work at the Inn, so he left me at Sam's boat. I sneaked through the trees so I could see my house and, sure enough, the Sheriff's SUV was out front.

I patted my pockets for my phone, and I remembered I had Reggie's Rastacap and my phone on my head. I looked at the phone.

There were two more messages from my mother and none from Sam. I felt my breath go out when I didn't hear from Sam and a kind of sick feeling when I saw those messages from my mother. I was sorry my mother had to deal with this shit.

> **"Sheriff called. Boat missing. Wants to know if we heard from you. Hope u r not involved."**
>
> **"Your father is so angry. Did you take money from his golf bag?"**

I started to feel bad about Joel being pissed and probably ragging my mother about what a loser I was, but then the helicopter flew overhead. I supposed it was a big deal for a Sheriff to have his boat stolen. I was sorry he had to go through this, too.

I went down into Sam's cabin and looked at my list on my phone. My next big thing: At 2 p.m. I needed to keep Officer Hultz busy so she'd miss the cremation.

Just to make myself feel better, I texted Sam even though I didn't think she'd answer.

> **"Hi. Where r u? We hid Pinkie. Boar cremation at 2 p.m. Need something to keep Hultz away from there. Reggie stole Sheriff's boat because you have his.**

I stopped and thought. Did I want to say more? I started typing again:

> **"Burial tonight. Need to figure out how to get Pinkie to the Big Banyan and how to dig in shell mound. If I do this and you aren't there, is there something special I should say?"**

I stopped again to think.

> **"Anyway, that's it. I miss you."**

And then:

> **"PS: I believe you are a Calusa."**

After I sent the message I felt my stomach gurgle and I had a pop tart and a Yoo-hoo. While I ate, I grabbed one of Sam's Calusa books from the shelf above the table. I thought it might have some stuff in it about spirit animal funerals. But first I needed to deal with Officer Hultz.

**8:00 a.m.**

1. Shark attack.
2. Panther stalking the children's pool at one of the country clubs.
3. Osprey (an angry-looking bird, sort of a small eagle) attacking someone's dog.

I studied my list. Any of these could get Officer Hultz to skip the cremation. But the list was stupid. How could I make any of this happen before 2 p.m.?

Just then, my phone text-chimed. I knew it was Sam. I looked at the screen. It wasn't Sam. It was from Jordan Minch:

> **"Yo Mop-Midget, need my $20. Going to dog races today. Bring it."**

My first thought was that I couldn't believe Jordan heard T. Rex call me Mop Midget. *Now that would get around the Sped Shed. Shit.*

I got on my bike and headed to Jordan's to give him his money. I had other things to do, but I didn't want him mad at me.

On my way, I passed the school and the Sped Shed and, as usual, a couple of tourists stood there next to a car from Iowa and looked in the drainage ditch for the alligator. I could have told them they were wasting their time, the alligator only came out in the aft…

THE ALLIGATOR!

I had my diversion. I knew what I was going to do.

I pedaled faster. I wondered if Nokoomis had spoken to me.

**8:30 a.m.**

You could see what all that beer the night before did to Jordan. The cherry picker was parked on top of a pile of gravel in his front yard. Jordan must have run it up there when he got home and just left it.

He stood in his driveway next to a pick-up. One of his brothers was in the truck, drinking a morning beer. I could hear some heavy bass from some music playing in there. Jordan's hair was all slicked down, and he had on some awful men's cologne. I mean, I could smell it even over the manure in his yard.

"Nice hat, Bob Marley."

At first I didn't know what Jordan was talking about, but then I remembered I still had Reggie's Rastacap on. I touched it but didn't take it off.

Jordan stuck his hand out, and when I gave him the last of Joel's stash—a twenty—he smiled and stuck the bill in the front pocket of his jeans. "Nice doin' business with ya." He opened the truck door.

"Uh, Jordan, I need a chicken."

The chickens were still running around Jordan's crappy front yard.

He turned back to me and closed the door. He looked a little confused, but interested.

"A chicken?"

"Yeah."

He leaned closer to me and whispered. "They're my brother's

chickens. What do you want it for?"

I tried to think about what would impress Jordan so he'd let me have a chicken. I imagined what they'd say in a movie. "I need it to make an impression on some people." I tried to keep my voice low and dangerous.

He nodded, and I knew this was going to cost me. That asshat Jordan thought I was a walking ATM machine. He glanced toward his brother who had the truck running, the windows up and the rap thumping. He wasn't going to hear us.

"Another twenty. And don't grab the chicken 'til we're gone."

I thought about bargaining on the price with him, but I didn't even have the money on me so I just nodded. My voice low again. "Fine. Pay you when the deal's done."

Jordan looked like he wanted to argue about not getting his chicken-money right away, but then I could tell he remembered it wasn't even his chicken and if his brother found out he was selling his chicken he'd probably beat the shit out of him, so he just shut up about that. He just got in the truck and they drove away.

I stood there alone in Jordan's front yard and looked at the chickens running around. I even made a half-assed grab at one of them when it zoomed by. I didn't get near it.

It was a good idea if I could make it work. How was I going to catch one of those chickens?

**9:00 a.m.**

I needed Reggie. I rode my bike back to the center of town.

There were chairs in the field behind the school and the stage with a sign behind it: "Heritage Day Dog Walk."

They have a big parade in the afternoon and a dinner at night, but in the morning they do this dog walk. Everybody lines up with their dogs—and they don't have to be special dogs—and they decorate them with ribbons and bows and little suits and shit. It must be really embarrassing to be a dog in that parade. Anyway, they dress them all up and walk around town and some people are the judges and they sit on stage and give out stupid awards. I know it sounds lame, but that's what you do when you live on an island.

Two ladies sat behind a registration table. Their dogs were tied up next to them. There was a big white poodle with a red bow on its head and a little terrier kind of dog with a ballerina's skirt on.

I stopped my bike in front of the grocery store. I saw myself in the window, and I couldn't believe it. I knew I still had Reggie's cap on, but the rest of me was a mess. There was dried mud and other ocean gunk on my shorts and shoes. My t-shirt was back in the bayou. My face was dirty, and my arms and legs were, too. I looked like I was on a survival show. I thought about finding a place to clean up, but I needed to keep going.

I found Reggie blowing leaves around near the Inn. The first thing he said when he saw me ride up on my bike was, "Oh no, Mon. I got work t' do. Don't be playin' wit Reggie." And then he got this big smile on his face. "Dat cap. It looks good on you, Mon."

I pulled my bike right up next to his golf cart, got off, and stood on the side away from the road in case the Sheriff drove by. I noticed the helicopter wasn't flying over anymore. Maybe they'd found his boat, but I didn't know if the Sheriff would still be looking for me. I mean, he got his boat back, right?

I decided to take the direct approach and tell Reggie exactly what I wanted him to do. It was too late for funning around. "I need you to help me catch a chicken."

**9:30 a.m.**

Reggie didn't even need convincing. He took a look around, got in his cart, and told me to throw my bike in the back. Five minutes later we stood in Jordan's front yard. There were three white chickens and one bigger one, which was red. They were racing each other around the yard in a big circle.

"Woo-ee, Mon. Dems are fast chickens. Don't know how we be catchin' dem."

This was another surprise about Reggie. First, I learned he couldn't swim, then I find out he didn't know how to catch a chicken. I thought all Jamaicans could swim and they use chickens for Voodoo and stuff. But I guess that's just a stereotype. I mean, I'm a white kid from Connecticut. Jamaicans probably think we all play polo and lacrosse.

"What you doin' wit a chicken, Wendell Wolf?"

I studied the chickens as I spoke. "Alligators eat chickens."

Reggie just looked at me. He didn't believe I knew this.

"I saw it on Discovery." He still didn't look convinced. "And a James Bond movie."

"Ah," he said and he nodded. (Apparently Jamaicans watch James Bond movies, too.) "So we wants de fat one."

I hadn't thought of that. One white chicken was a lot fatter than the others.

"But I need a fast chicken, one that can get away from the alligator."

Reggie shook his head. "Mon, I thought you just said you wanted de gator to eat...."

"That one." I pointed to the red one.

"Dat one's a rooster."

I guess Reggie did know something about chickens. The rooster was bigger than the other chickens, and he sort of strutted around the yard. He looked like what I needed.

Reggie went the side of the house and came back with a rake and a big red plastic washtub. He handed the tub to me. "Rooster's mean. Watch d' spurs on his legs." Then he circled the yard to get on the other side of the rooster. I stood there with the tub. Reggie had the rake and I had the tub. I guess I knew what I was supposed to do.

Reggie moved slowly so the rooster was trapped against a hedge and he had nowhere to go except toward me. The rooster wasn't happy. I could tell it when his "clucks" changed to "squawks." Reggie's voice was low as he talked to the rooster. "Come on, Mr. Rooster, just a bit more." And then to me, "Get down low. When he runs, get him in d' tub."

I never knew roosters could run that fast. All of a sudden, he took off toward me and I jumped forward with the tub. Reggie yelled, "Get him." When the rooster saw the tub coming, he veered off away from the hedge. I landed on my hands and knees and the tub rolled away.

The rooster tried to get by Reggie, but Reggie shifted the rake to his other hand and blocked him. The rooster turned back toward me, and that's when I dove. I know I had my eyes closed, but somehow I caught him on one of his skinny legs right as my belly hit the ground and knocked the wind out of me.

At this point, there was a lot of flapping and squawking, Reggie yelling "Hold him!" and all sorts of pecking and scratching on my arms. I remember Reggie throwing something over both me and the rooster, and I remember thinking—because whatever he threw on me stunk—that it must have been the tarp from the manure pile. Then there was light and the scratching stopped. I looked up, and Reggie had the rooster in a bundle in the tarp in his arms.

He gave me one of his big grins. "Woo-ee, Wendell Wolf. You tackle dat rooster like a big panther!"

Reggie held the squirming bundle tight against his chest. "I tink I gots sometin' in d' cart to carry him wit'." Reggie headed over to his cart on the road.

I pulled myself up into a sitting position and got my phone out of my shorts pocket to check for messages from Sam. Nothing. I had the big sinking feeling again.

All of a sudden I was so tired. I looked down and saw I had big scratches on my arms and bloody pecks on my hands. Then I thought about my plan for the rooster and that it was stupid, and that made me more tired and I wanted to cry again. I didn't want Reggie to see, so I kind of turned sideways to wipe my eyes with the back of my hand. My eyes stung, and I looked at my hands. They were really filthy. And now my eyes were running because of some crap I had on my hands. And then my nose started to run. I stood there with tears and snot running down my face feeling like a fool.

I felt Reggie's arm around my shoulders. "It's OK, Mon. You been workin' hard. You deserve a little boo-hoo."

I struggled to my feet and pulled away from him. I felt light-headed, and I thought I was going to puke. "I'm not crying, I got stuff in my eyes from my hands." But then I really felt stupid because now my face looked like I was crying and that made me actually start to cry for real.

"Check 'dis, Mon." He showed me the rooster, which he had bundled in a towel and tied up with some yellow nylon rope. The bundle squirmed around and made an angry squawking noise. I know he was proud and he was trying to make me feel better, but I just bent over and put my hands on my knees. I heard him move away.

I stayed that way until I felt Reggie next to me again and he put his arm back on my shoulders. In front of me he held out a Red Bull and I took it.

"Here, Mon. Sip dis. Wendell Wolf, he need a little pick-me-up."

That made me feel better until he said, "Sammy-girl be proud of you."

That made me cry some more. I felt like a dork.

After a minute or so, I stood up straight and drank the whole Red Bull. I was really thirsty, plus it gave me something to do while my face dried off.

We walked over to the cart. Reggie said, "Mon, sorry to say 'dis, but I needs to get d' cart back to d' Inn. They be missin' it and Reggie soon." I was still pretty tired, and I was still thinking about Sam so I didn't really understand what he was saying.

But then, he pulled my bike out of the cart and set it on the road and reached back in and grabbed the rooster bundle (which squawked) and handed it to me. He smiled, "Good luck, Mon." And he drove away.

I just stood there holding that squirming, squawking rooster in the towel. I used the corner of the towel to wipe the blood off my arms and my hands. Carefully, I got on my bike and I held the rooster-bundle in one hand while I tried to hold on to the handlebar with the other.

I managed to make it back to town on my bike, but it wasn't easy. I stayed on a bike path because I was a mess, still wearing the Rastacap with my clothes covered in dirt.

I passed a couple of people walking their dressed-up dogs to the Dog Walk. The rooster was still squawking and flopping around in the towel, but I kept my head down and pedaled.

**10:30 a.m.**

I leaned my bike against the big Gumbo Limbo tree next to the Sped Shed.

On the other side of the school, I could hear them warming up the microphone for the Dog Walk, but there was nobody around near the ditch. I grabbed two leaves off a palm tree, then I slid down in the ditch next to the pipe. I used the light on my phone to check in the pipe for the gator. Nothing. (Luckily)

I got down in the ditch water so my body blocked the pipe, and I put the towel with the rooster in it in front of me with the tied end toward the pipe. Carefully, I untied Reggie's knot in the yellow rope. When the rooster felt me doing this, he started jumping around like crazy. All of a sudden the knot came undone, the towel came loose, and the rooster popped his head out and looked around. I panicked and grabbed under the towel and shoved it and the rooster into the pipe and then I stuffed the two palm leaves in after it. There. Plugged. I heard a squawk or two from the pipe, but then nothing.

I looked around. Nobody saw me. OK.

**Noon**

I didn't know what to expect, and that gave me all sorts of thoughts.

I mean, would the gator smell the rooster and run down the pipe? What if the gator was in a pipe on the other side of town? What if he was in one of the ponds on the golf course? How far did rooster smell travel? I hadn't thought this plan through.

I had time to think about all this, because I sat down next to my bike and the Gumbo Limbo to wait. I could hear a band playing in the distance. The bike path was filled with dogs and people, all dressed up and decorated.

"Wendell, is that you?" It was a simple question but I could hear the tone: "What are *you* doing here?" And, "Why do you look like shit?"

I looked around. *Dammit.* I was right. It was Missy Buckler and a bunch of the DQs. Every one of them was dressed up like their dog.

Missy had a little fluffy white dog, it had a little pirate's hat on, and Missy had on the same kind of hat, only bigger. Her dog started sniffing the rooster smell on my hand, and I pulled it away.

She stood in front of me and looked down. "Nice hat. Where's your dog?" At first I didn't know what she was talking about, but then I remembered I was wearing Reggie's Rastacap.

I tried to play like I was there for the parade. "Uh, he's on his way…uh...." My mind went blank. I didn't even own a dog. I was tired and my head buzzed. "Uh, my mom's bringing him." I thought that sounded lame. "Uh, today's his day for…uh…protection training." I thought that sounded stupid when it came out but it had a nice effect on Missy—a combination of confusion and disgust. She didn't know what "protection" meant, but she probably was seeing my non-existent Doberman ripping the shit out of a leather glove on some trainer's hand.

"Ri-ght." Missy said this in two syllables, like she didn't believe me, but it was a signal for the rest of the DQ's to make snorting noises, turn, and walk away. "You need a shower, by the way." Missy said that over her shoulder, and her tribe laughed. Just like the DQ's; one final shot. *Idiots.*

I sat there a little longer, thinking about the pipe, the rooster, and the alligator. Could that rooster get out the other end? It was a drainpipe, so where would it drain? Toward the ocean?

I jumped up and got on my bike and pedaled over to the beach. And there it was, an open drainpipe. It was dry, but I figured that was because it hadn't rained lately. There were people on the beach, so I pretended to be casual and sat down next to the pipe, like a guy who comes to a beautiful beach to sit next to a drainpipe. I backed up so my ear was close to the pipe. Did I hear squawking?

I sat back and thought about it. Who knew what was going on inside that pipe? Maybe the rooster met the alligator and they were hanging out, making friends. Maybe the alligator wasn't even in the pipe. *Shit. Couldn't I do anything right?*

I decided I needed to block up that end of the pipe. I couldn't have the gator and the rooster escape onto the beach. For my plan to work, it had to happen at the other end of the pipe, where all the people were. I looked around the beach and found what I needed, an old crab trap in the sand. (It's like a wire box about the size of a small suitcase that fishermen use to catch crabs.) Sometimes storms blow them up onto the beach. With a lot of pushing and bending, I jammed it in the end of the pipe.

Now I needed to get back to where I'd stuffed in the rooster.

**12:30 p.m.**

I rode my bike as fast as I could through town, trying to figure out how my drainage pipe plan was going to work.

I know I wasn't watching where I was going, that was the first problem.

The second problem was the speed bump. The stupid islanders let anybody—well, almost anybody—kids, tourists, people with kids on their laps, teenagers—drive golf carts. Instead of telling some of them they can't drive, the islanders put speed bumps in the road to slow everybody down. Which probably works except they are really dangerous when you're riding your bike fast and don't see one coming.

I ended up on my back in a palmetto. It's this plant with spiky leaves, but the problem is, the leaves have little teeth on them like a saw.

I was mainly cut on my legs with one big scratch on my knee. Anyway, there was a lot of blood, and me on my back right in the middle of all the people getting ready to do the Dog Walk.

I don't think I passed out or anything, but when I opened my eyes there were people standing around me. I got to my feet and brushed myself off and everybody went back to what they were doing. "Just a crazy teenager on his bike. He looks OK."

I walked a couple of steps and my knee hurt bad, but I left my bike and walked to the pipe near the Sped Shed and collapsed under the Gumbo Limbo. One cut on my leg looked pretty deep so I got another palm leaf and wrapped it around my shin. I sat there and didn't really know what to do. It hurt to walk, and now my back and head hurt, too. My bike was still in the palmetto, and I couldn't ride it because it had a bent front wheel. *Farming speed bump.*

I heard someone running up behind me, and Missy Buckler leaned down into my face.

"Wendell. Thank God you're still here. Could you, um, do us, um, a big favor?"

Missy held her little pirate dog in her arms. Behind Missy there was another DQ with tears running down her face. She pulled a small Chihuahua along on a leash. "Shannon forgot Pepe's costume, and she wants to be in the parade anyhow? Do you think you could hold her dog for her?"

I tried to think. It was all so weird. Leave it to a DQ to want to walk in the Dog Walk parade without her dog.

"Yeah." The old Wendell said that. The Wendell that wanted the DQ's to like him. The new Wendell had things to do, namely, get an alligator to chase a rooster out of a pipe and later, bury a pig. I tried to get out of it. "Look, Missy, I'm really busy."

"Thanks, Wendell." She grabbed the leash from Shannon, pulled Pepe the Chihuahua through some loose gravel, and handed Pepe to me. Then the two of them hurried away. After a couple of steps, Missy yelled over her shoulder, "Your leg is bleeding."

I just sat there, waiting. Nothing happened at the pipe. I was getting desperate.

I felt my phone vibrate. It was a message from T. Rex:

**"WTF r u doing? Hultz firing up the oven."**

I told Mr. Sanders I'd tell the truth when I wrote this, even when I looked bad. This is one of those times. I don't really have any excuses, except I really wanted to help Sam and I really wanted to finish what we had started. I needed to get Officer Hultz out of the shelter.

I picked Pepe up, unhooked his leash, and limped down to the beach. I know I didn't have a shirt on and I know I was all scratched up and bloody (rooster and palmetto), but when people saw me, they must have thought I was part of the parade or something. You know, like a bloody pirate with his dog.

I made it to the beach and the drainage pipe, and I looked around. Nobody saw me. Quickly, I pulled the crab trap out of the pipe and threw Pepe in. I know. It makes me look terrible. But now I had a Chihuahua in there to chase the rooster toward the gator. It was all I could think of.

**1:00 p.m.**

I limped as fast as I could back through town to the drainage pipe by the Sped Shed.

They blew the siren on a fire truck to start the Dog Walk. That wasn't a great idea, because all the dogs started barking and running around. When their owners got them all settled and back in line, they started the parade. The parade route was supposed to be a square, down Banyan Street to Park Street, then down School Street to the bike path and the Sped Shed, then down the bike path back to the Community Center. Along the streets, people stood in their yards and waved and shouted as everybody walked by with their dogs.

On my way past the Community Center, I slowed down and acted like I was looking at a rack of clothes outside Banyan Bargains. When no one was looking, I stole a shirt, white with a little gold sheep on it. It looked like what Joel wore golfing.

For a second, I wondered how many crimes I'd committed in the past 24 hours.

I heard it before I saw it. There was a lot of yelling and extra barking up at the corner. But there was laughing, too. It sounded like they were having a good time. Then somebody's German shepherd ran past me dragging its leash and a little wagon. I heard some lady yelling, "Fritz, heel, Fritz."

Finally I got to the big circle of people. They were looking in the ditch next to the drainage pipe. I saw what they were looking at. My red rooster was charging around, but it wasn't running away, it was squawking and doing circles around the alligator. Every time it ran past, it pecked the gator. Every time it pecked, the gator tried to bite it, but missed. Every time the gator missed, it must have been pissed off because it hissed and spit.

On the outside, Pepe the Chihuahua chased the rooster and yipped, but he stayed back a safe distance because the rooster kept turning and pecking at it, too.

The people in the big circle of people didn't seem worried. They were having fun.

I couldn't believe it. My plan worked. These people were in DANGER.

I pulled out my phone. 1:35 p.m. I had the Animal Shelter number in my favorites list. I hit "Call."

"Shelter." T. Rex answered. I lowered my voice and I tried to sound urgent.

"Uh, there's a...uh…." My mind went blank. I couldn't believe I wasn't ready for this. "Uh…a…."

T. Rex's voice came back. "An ANIMAL problem?" He said it

really loud, and I got the message.

"Yeah. An ANIMAL problem. A BIG animal problem." I was warming up. I could hear T. Rex repeating. "A BIG animal problem? Yes, that does sound like a big problem."

I got into it. "Yeah, I think people's lives might be in danger. It's a GATOR."

I thought I heard T. Rex choke back a laugh. "Lives are in danger. A HUGE gator?"

Now I started to laugh. I decided to add something good. "I think you should send Officer Hultz."

T. Rex came back to me. "Yes, we'll send SOMEBODY." I got what I did wrong. The average caller to the animal shelter wouldn't request Officer Hultz by name.

T. Rex fixed that. "Well, that sounds like a matter for Officer Hultz. She'll respond as soon as possible." And then he paused. "I'll have to take over for her here." That was a message to me. When Hultz left the shelter, he'd cremate the boar. Hultz wouldn't know they cooked the wrong pig. Was it going to work? I didn't know. But I gave it my best shot.

A minute later, I saw Sheriff Pruitt drive up in his SUV. I stayed back, pulled the cap lower on my head, and stepped behind the Gumbo Limbo.

Smiling, the Sheriff walked up to the big circle of owners and dogs. He thought the whole thing was pretty funny. By this time, most of the dogs stopped barking and people pulled them in on their leashes. The gator just sat there in the grass in the sun. It had its eyes closed like it was enjoying itself. Missy's friend Shannon finally showed up, holding Pepe and talking in his ear.

"So, what's going on?" Sheriff Pruitt didn't say this to anyone, really. It was like he just walked into a picnic or something, and he was asking about the weather. He looked into the ditch.

"The gator, huh?" Sheriff Pruitt was pretty cool, like he was talking about what he had for lunch.

Everybody started talking at once. Sheriff Pruitt listened and nodded like he understood and really *was* concerned. Then when people's voices calmed down, he walked over and picked up one of the palm leaves the alligator must have pushed out the end of the pipe. He stepped down near the gator and brushed its tail with the leaf, and the gator hissed and walked slowly over to the pipe, went inside and disappeared. Sheriff Pruitt dropped the leaf next to the ditch and wiped his hands on his pants. "There."

There was total silence, even from the dogs. I think they were disappointed their fun was over. Shannon sniffed and hugged Pepe, who looked embarrassed.

Above me, I heard a squawk and looked up. The rooster was high up in the tree watching everything. I didn't know roosters could fly.

In the distance, I heard a siren. It got louder as it got closer. I saw the lights as Hultz's Animal Control cart screeched around the corner and skidded to a stop on some gravel. The siren stopped, and Officer Hultz jumped her big ass off the driver's seat. Then she leaned in the back of the cart, pulled her pants up in back, and turned back around with her rifle. "What's going on here?" Her voice was shaky, and her face was sweaty. She held the gun up like you see soldiers do in ceremonies.

"All taken care of, Officer Hultz." Sheriff Pruitt sounded a lot tenser than he had before. He was probably afraid Hultz was going to shoot someone.

Hultz stepped down toward the ditch, and she slipped a bit. "I received a report that lives were in danger." She looked around, and she seemed angry that there wasn't anything going on.

Then some girl in the crowd—I think it was Missy or Shannon, because she had a Valley Girl voice—said, "It was a HUGE alligator." Then everybody talked at once. "Six feet long." "Attacked the Chihuahua." "Sharp teeth."

Sheriff Pruitt leaned down and said something in Officer Hultz's ear, and she lowered her gun. Then Sheriff Pruitt took it out of her shaking hands. In a loud voice she said, "All right, everything's fine here, go about your business."

That seemed to do it for everyone, because the parade organizers started yelling for everyone to get back in line.

Sheriff Pruitt climbed out of the ditch, shook hands with a couple of adults, and headed back to his SUV, carrying Officer Hultz's gun.

I got my phone out and checked the time. It was 2:15 p.m.

I texted T. Rex:

**"?"**

He texted me:

**"Boar BBQ."**

It worked. T. Rex cremated the wrong pig and Officer Hultz didn't know.

## Sam Comes Back

I was at the picnic table. My leg hurt from my fall off the bike into the palmetto, and I was really tired because I'd been up all night. Plus I was hungry and thirsty. And pissed. And sad. I remembered the last text I sent Sam and how I asked if she kissed me because she liked me or wanted me to do stuff for her. She never answered. I felt like an idiot. And now I really didn't want to know.

I really didn't know how to bury Pinkie on the golf course. Everything just closed in on me.

I just gave up. I stood up and felt a little dizzy, and I decided to go home and face the wrath of my mom and the indifference of Joel. Sam could figure out the rest of it herself. When she got back. *If* she got back. Maybe her sketchy spirit Nokoomis would help.

Walking up my driveway, I took off Reggie's stupid Rastacap and threw it in the bushes. I wondered if Joel's Escalade still stunk. I counted the days. Today was Saturday. We'd picked up the dead boar two days ago on Thursday. A lot had happened since then, but yes, Joel's stupid Escalade probably still stunk.

I noticed the driveway was empty. Good. That meant Joel was golfing. At least I didn't have to listen to his bullshit.

Then I stopped. I really didn't know why. It was this weird feeling. I needed to finish this. I wanted to help Sam. I pushed my way into the bushes next to the driveway, found Reggie's cap, and put it back on.

I sat back down at the picnic table and put my head on my hands to think. I woke up when I felt the table creak and sink a little. I lifted my head, and Sam was sitting across from me, right there, just looking at me. First, I wondered if I was dreaming. Then, I put my head back down, because I didn't want her to see me cry.

I felt the table move when she got up, and I still kept my head down. Maybe it was a dream. I couldn't believe she was leaving. I felt more tears on my arms.

Then I felt the table sink on my side and her arm across my shoulders. I still didn't want to lift my head because now I was crying even more.

(Mr. Sanders, can we take some of this crying stuff out?)

We just sat there like that with Sam holding me tight. Finally I looked up, and she pulled a wad of Kleenex out of her pocket and wiped my face. Then she licked the Kleenex and wiped my face again. "You're a mess."

I laughed a little and looked at her more closely. Her hair was all tumbled around and it wasn't shiny like it usually was. Her face had dried salt spray on it. You could tell she'd been out on the water in a fast boat. I sniffed a little. She had B.O. It wasn't bad, but it was there. I took her Kleenex, licked it, and wiped her face, too.

After that we just sat there next to each other without saying anything. Both of us had our heads down. Finally, I couldn't stand it any longer so I spoke. "I didn't know where you were." This sounded neutral to me. I was still really mad at her and hurt that she left me.

"I had to go away."

I thought about this. She was neutral, too. I sat there for a while. I guess I wanted to get her to apologize. I thought about telling her she really hurt my feelings, but that sounded really lame. But I hated the silence.

Finally, I said, "I know." This sounded dumb, but it was all I could think of.

Sam sat there with her head bowed. There were two ospreys circling overhead, whistling at each other. One of them had a fish, and the other wanted it.

"Where did you go?" I asked this because it didn't sound like she was going to say she was sorry. I thought I might as well get some information.

"To find my family."

"Where?" She just shrugged and didn't answer. I was looking at the top of her bowed head, and I was getting frustrated. Plus, my palmetto cuts hurt and I was thirsty.

"Did you find them?"

With that, she looked up. "Look, Wendell, I was having a bad time. I went somewhere to find some things out. Now I'm back. I'm sorry. But, I read every one of your texts and you did great on your own."

There was another silence. Here's a list of what I thought:

1. Did she go see some guy? (I know. Pathetic.)
2. Was she still a Calusa? Was there a Nokoomis?
3. She read my texts and she thinks I did great.
4. She apologized.
5. And, she called me "Wendell." That was my post-kiss name. Not "Wolf," but "Wendell." I felt pretty good about hearing that.

She looked down at my legs. "You've got some bad cuts, there. Let's get you cleaned up."

We both stood up. I guess that conversation was over.

**2:30 p.m.**

It felt so good when Sam rubbed my legs that I couldn't keep my eyes open. I was on the floor of her cabin on a towel, and Sam was next to me. She made me lie there when she poured this bubbly stuff out of a brown bottle on my cuts and then patted it dry with a paper towel. I was almost asleep when I felt Sam's boat shift, and then there was a soft tapping on the door to her cabin.

Now my eyes were wide open, and Sam's were, too. She held a finger to her lips for me to be quiet. There was a whisper from outside, "Sammy Girl?"

Sam looked at me and mouthed, "Reggie." And then she got up and let him in.

Reggie stepped down into the cabin and looked at me on the floor. I had band-aids all over my legs, and I must have looked pretty pathetic. He just shook his head and smiled. Then he grabbed Sam by the neck with both hands and played like he was going to strangle her. "Sammy-girl, where you go in my boat?"

Sam just laughed and pulled away. She wasn't going to tell Reggie where she went, either, but Reggie didn't seem to care.

Then, taking turns, Reggie and I told Sam about everything we had done. I told her how Jordan and I substituted the boar for Pinkie and how I had to help T. Rex shave the boar. Then Reggie told her about moving Pinkie onto the island. "We—Wendell Wolf and me—we had to use d' Sheriff's boat and woo-ee, what a ruckus." He grinned down at me. "But we got it done, tanks to Wendell here." He laughed loudly. "I never forget d' sight of dat boy wadin' down d' canal, pushin' ole Pinkie." And then he laughed even louder.

Then, I told Reggie and Sam about creating the diversion at the dog walk, and I made both of them laugh when I told them about the Chihuahua and the alligator and Sheriff Pruitt taking the gun away from Officer Hultz.

We were done, and it was quiet. The boat rocked a little as another boat passed by on the canal. I watched Sam to see if she had a reaction to the story. I really wanted her to be proud of me. And it was almost like she read my mind. First, she kissed Reggie on the cheek. Then, she reached her hand down to me, pulled me to my feet, and when I was standing, she grabbed me in a really tight, full-body hug. And then she kissed me on the lips. Really kissed me. On the lips. And she let me go and looked right in my eyes, right in front of Reggie and said, "I love you, Wendell."

Reggie brought in some Red Bulls from his golf cart, and Sam pulled out some pop tarts. That gave us a burst of energy. The three of us sat at Sam's table.

As usual, I waited for Sam to start. Instead, she looked at me and said, "What are we going to do?"

Reggie and I just sat there. I mean, yeah, we did all that stuff, but now that Sam was back, wasn't she going to be in charge like she always was? Was she still a Calusa? Were we still talking to Nokoomis? I was filled with questions.

Instead of asking, I untaped my list from her wall and spread it out on the table.

#1 on the list: Bury Pinkie by midnight.

All of a sudden, Sam got a text, and she smiled and stood up. "I have a surprise for you. We need to go down to the bayou."

**3:00 p.m.**

Right after that, everything turned to shit.

The three of us were in Reggie's cart, leaving the marina. I was pretty excited about Sam's surprise, but even more excited because Sam was sitting on my lap in the front (only two seats in the cart, good for me!). I said something about holding tight, and I put my arms around Sam from behind. She had her shorts on and her bare legs on mine made me shiver a little. I'm sure both Reggie and Sam knew I didn't need to hold on to Sam, but nobody said anything.

I don't know why Reggie went out the front entrance to the marina, but I was so happy about Sam on my lap, I wasn't paying attention.

Officer Hultz stood in my driveway, next to her cart, talking to Joel and my mother. She looked up, looked surprised, and jumped out into the street and waved us over.

We had to stop. Caught. We couldn't get around her. What could we do? Make a run for it in a golf cart?

**3:30 p.m.**

First, Hultz let Reggie leave. It was obvious it was Sam and me they were after.

We sat in a circle around the living room.

My mom offered everyone drinks and Joel—dressed as usual in plaid golf pants and a shirt with Banyan Inn on it—said it was almost cocktail hour. He went in the alcove and made himself a drink. On his way back into the room, he grabbed Reggie's Rastacap off my head and threw it in my lap. "Take that stupid thing off."

Officer Hultz sat on one of my mom's wooden antique dining room chairs and made it groan.

Sam and I sat next to each other on the couch, and I scooted over next to her so our legs touched. (I know, this is pathetic to remember.)

Joel sat down in his favorite chair, took a big sip of his drink, and started in. He yelled at me for maybe ten minutes. I zoned out after a while, but some of the words came through. " Embarrassment." "No potential." "No self-control." "Russian bastard." "Not going to ruin Heritage Day." "Don't know what the two of you are up to."

I looked at my mom once, and she looked down. No help there.

Finally Joel wound down, mainly because he had to get up and get himself another drink.

While he was gone, nobody said anything, but Officer Hultz blasted out a big smoker's cough. Even though the house was air-conditioned (Joel liked it as cold as a freezer), Hultz was sweating.

As I watched her, something bothered me. She was really nervous. I wondered why Hultz was there and not Pruitt.

And then it came to me. Hultz was there because of the riot I'd caused with the alligator and all the other stuff that had happened the past couple of days. It was Heritage Day. Heritage Day and the Inn. Joel just said, "Not going to ruin Heritage Day." Hultz worked for the Inn. She was there to protect the Inn's image.

This was also about Joel and the Inn. He wanted to make a good impression on Pugsley. He hated Granger's, and he didn't know what Sam and I were doing. This was his big night, and he was afraid I was going to ruin it. He and Hultz were trying to scare us. We weren't going to jail.

All of a sudden, I had to pee. Maybe I was relieved, but it just came over me. I told everybody where I was going, and I got up to use the bathroom off the hall.

I remember what happened next in a sort of slow motion.

On my way back into the living room, I passed in back of Joel in his recliner.

He took a sip of his drink, swallowed, and put the glass down on the table. Then he said to Hultz, "This is all because of that Indian slut."

He was talking about Sam. I looked at her. She looked like someone punched her in the stomach.

All of a sudden all I could see was red. My head hurt, and I was kind of fuzzy behind my eyes. I had a hard time breathing.

And I hit him.

It was on the back of his head, and it was the back of my hand, kind of a back-handed slap.

I just lost control of my hand. Just like the thing with Greggy when I saw red before I bit him. But it wasn't a bite this time, it was a hit, or a slap. Or something.

It sure surprised everybody. Most of all, Joel. He screamed like he'd been gored by a water buffalo.

**5:15 p.m.**

I woke up in a bed with railings on it. There were water stains on the ceiling. The room had curtains on the windows, so I couldn't see outside. It was sort of dark in there, and I had a really bad headache. And I was alone.

Stuff started coming back to me. I needed to get Pinkie Pie. And bury her by midnight. *Where was I?* Without moving my head, I felt around for my phone and found it on the table next to the bed. I held it over my face and I saw it was 5:15 p.m. That made me feel a little better. At least I hadn't been asleep too long. Just to be sure, I checked the date. Saturday, September 15. OK, it was the same day.

I felt something weird going on with my other arm, and I lifted it. There was a tube stuck in the back of my hand going up to a plastic bag with liquid in it hanging from a stand. *Was I in a hospital?*

Then a dream came back to me. Me seeing red. That same hand, the one now with the tube in it, moving through the air, disconnected from my body. The smack sound on the back of Joel's bald head.

I closed my eyes.

**5:30 p.m.**

I woke up, and when I tried to lift my head, it hurt like a bitch. Then I felt a hand on my arm. It was rough and warm, and I knew it was Sam's. Slowly, I turned my head that way. She looked down at me with her black eyes wide.

Seeing her made me start to cry. My head hurt and I was confused.

"What happened?" My voice felt weird, kind of hoarse.

Her voice was quiet, almost a whisper. "After you slapped your dad, your eyes rolled back in your head and you kind of crumpled to the floor." She put a cool cloth on my forehead.

"Where am I?"

"In the Island Clinic. Since it's the weekend, they want you to stay over until Monday when the doctor is here." She leaned over and wiped my eyes with a tissue.

Then it was quiet. I focused on what Sam had said. *The Island Clinic?* The Island Clinic was a one-room cottage next to the Community Center where they gave old people flu shoots and took their blood pressure. I didn't even know they had beds in the Island Clinic. *I fainted or whatever, and they took me to the Island Clinic? WTF? Not even to a hospital? And they don't even have a doctor here until Monday?*

But my head really hurt. I was also confused and floating. I wondered what kind of medicine was dripping into me from that bag. "Where are my mom and Joel?" I asked.

Sam was quiet for a second before she answered. "They went to the Heritage Day dinner."

I closed my eyes, and I could feel the tears. I hoped the tears would stay under my eyelids so Sam wouldn't see them. Their only kid gets taken to the hospital, and Joel and my mom go to a dinner. Figures.

Sam broke the silence. "But *I'm* here." I opened my eyes and looked at her. "And thank you for standing up for me." She kissed me on the forehead.

**6:00 p.m.**

The door to the room opened. I saw his dreadlocks first as his head poked around the door. It was Reggie.

His big grin made me feel better. "Mon, you look like you gonna live after all. Sammy-Girl texted me. Dis boy hit his old man? Woo-ee!" And he laughed hard, that great Reggie-laugh. Sam joined in, so I did too, and when I stopped, I noticed my head didn't hurt so much.

All of a sudden I felt something under the sheet. Or, really, I didn't feel anything.

"They took your shorts," Sam said with a big smile.

I was wearing just my underwear. "Why?"

"Because your shorts were filthy and bloody, and apparently they don't like that in their beds around here."

"Who took my shorts off?"

Her grin got even wider. "We did."

"We?"

"The nurse undid your belt, I pulled down your shorts."

I didn't really care about the nurse seeing me in my underwear, but

I worried about what Sam saw. I tried to remember what underwear I had on. Jockeys or boxers? I liked jockeys, even though most guys wore boxers. Then I remembered I'd been up all night wading in a swamp. Whichever pair I wore, they weren't going to be pretty.

"Cute tighty-whities, by the way." Sam laughed, and that answered the question. But then she squeezed my hand and winked at me. Reggie couldn't stop laughing.

**6:20 p.m.**

The door opened again, and someone in an orange plastic vest walked in. I was still foggy from whatever they were dripping into me, and I didn't recognize him until he spoke. "Hey Mop-Midget. Where's the party?"

I knew it was T. Rex, but he looked different. His ponytail was stuck up under a hard hat. There were big letters on the back of his vest: "Traffic Control." I could see he had his Dead t-shirt on under the vest.

Of course Sam and Reggie knew about T. Rex, but he didn't know about them. So I had to explain who everybody was. It was strange to see the three of them together: Sam, a dark-skinned white girl with muscles...Reggie, a skinny Jamaican Rastafarian...and T. Rex, previously a hippie, an animal shelter worker, but now a traffic guard or something. And then there was me, a short white kid in a bed at the stupid Island Clinic.

I raised my head a little so I could see T. Rex better. "What are you doing here?"

T. Rex grinned. "Hultz has me parking cars at the club. She just called me and told me I had to be back at the shelter at 8:00 p.m. She told me what happened, and she's bragging she's coming over here with a big surprise for you, and that you're goin' to State Juvie until you're 21. Not even the Sheriff can save you, she says."

I felt Sam's hand tighten on my arm.

Then he continued. "Anyway, I snuck away early. Those rich pricks can park their own cars." He grinned and continued, "I just came over to see if you were OK."

I thought about that. It was nice he came to see me, but what was going on with Hultz?

Then Sam spoke, and her tone surprised the shit out of me. "Tell me how the cars are parked. Does the main aisle between the cars run north-south or east-west?" She sounded like a general asking her soldiers for information about the enemy.

*What was Sam up to?*

T. Rex held his hand up in the air and spread his fingers and thumb wide. Then he turned slowly around in a circle. "Uh, east-west, I think." He looked at Sam like a kid who wondered if he got a question right in school. He stopped and thought. "Except for the governor and a couple of the other big wigs. They had drivers and bodyguards. Their cars are in the circle in front of the Inn." He looked at me. "Your old man's Escalade is out there, right in the middle of everything."

All of a sudden it came back to me; before we got caught by Hultz, Sam had a surprise, and she was taking us somewhere in the golf cart. *Where was she taking us?*

**6:30 p.m.**

T. Rex left, and Sam went out in the hall with him.

A minute later, she came back in and tossed me a pair of scrub pants. I held them up. They were like huge pajamas.

"Let's go."

Just like that.

"But what about my headache?"

"You're all better. Come on, get your pants on. We've got a shitload to do by midnight." The old Sam was back.

"I'm supposed to stay in the hospital until Monday."

Sam rolled her eyes. "First of all, it's not a hospital. It's the stupid clinic…."

"But…."

"Wolf, sometimes you can be quite a titty-baby. If you had something serious, they would have taken you to the real hospital. They just wanted you out of the way so you wouldn't make trouble at the dinner."

"What about this?" I pointed to the needle in my arm and the bag on the stand.

"Sugar and salt water, Mon." Reggie pointed to a label on the bag. Then he reached down, pulled the adhesive tape off my hand, and gently pulled the needle out of my vein or artery or whatever it was stuck in. Then he opened a Band-Aid and put it where the needle was. "Dere, Mon, good as new." I shook my head. *How did Reggie know how to remove an IV?*

"Get your pants on." Sam was standing at the door looking down the hall.

"But...."

I was going to ask for some privacy, but she interrupted me. "We've already seen it Wolf. Hurry up, the hall's empty."

She was back to calling me "Wolf," which I didn't like. I threw off the sheet and pulled the scrubs over my jockeys. I was right. My underwear was really dirty.

Reggie helped me stand up. I wasn't dizzy, and my headache was gone. A miracle.

Another minute later, the three of us were behind a bush beside the clinic.

**6:45 p.m.**

First, Sam told Reggie he needed to go get a bigger cart and to meet us at her boat.

As soon as we got in her cabin, she kissed me. I mean, really kissed me. After a couple of minutes of serious tongue dancing, Sam stopped to breathe. "I'm so proud of you, I'm so happy you're OK." She put her lips back on mine, and when I hugged her around her waist, I felt her hand move to my butt, over the scrub pants. She squeezed me a little and whispered in my ear, "I love your undies, Wendell."

I felt a strange ache in my chest. She was back to calling me "Wendell."

We heard Reggie's maintenance cart skid in the gravel outside and felt his steps on the deck before we could move. Maybe that's because Sam was biting on my neck and squeezing my butt, but that's just a guess.

"Woo-ee, break it up, you two. We got a full night."

Sam pulled away from me and pulled down her t-shirt. I didn't remember doing anything with her shirt, but I saw the bottom of her white bra against her tan skin. My dizziness came back for just a second, until I shook my head.

Reggie sat down at the table and waited, smiling all the while. Sam moved around the cabin. All of a sudden it seemed like she was in a big hurry. I wondered if now was the time for her big surprise.

"OK, I need the two of you to take Reggie's cart to the Big Banyan. Reggie, you know what to do. Wendell, I need you to dig the hole under the tree."

I didn't understand. Hadn't I figured that out? Then I started again, "We can't dig under…."

For some reason, Sam was taking her Calusa stuff off the wall of her cabin. She had this feathered headdress in her hands. "Just roll with it. You'll figure it out when you get there."

Reggie drove the cart, and I sat beside him, quiet. In two minutes, we went from Sam nibbling on my neck and squeezing my butt to her giving me orders. Was this what being a boyfriend was like? She'd been missing and I'd done all the work. I was pretty confused. And pissed.

Reggie knew that, I guess. "Don't let it bother you, Mon. Sammy, she got a lot on her mind."

It still bothered me a little.

"Goin' to d' shop, first."

I shook my head. Apparently there were things going on that I didn't know about. I hoped we were getting some stuff to help me dig under the tree.

Reggie took us by the Inn to the maintenance shop in the back. On the way, I could see the lights from the dinner. The tables were set on the lawn where they play croquet. All the palm trees had those Japanese lanterns in them. Off to the side, they had a big outdoor kitchen under a tent where the food was prepared. There was an old people's kind of band with guys in tuxedos. It looked like it was still before dinner, people were standing around eating stuff from trays passed around by waiters and waitresses. Everyone wore pirate costumes, and the waiters all wore the same pirate hats.

Reggie drove the cart to the shed, got out, opened these big garage doors, drove in, and closed the doors. The shed was huge like an aircraft hangar, and there were these incredibly bright lights hanging from the ceiling. We were all alone in there, and our voices echoed.

"OK, Mon. I need help here." Reggie pulled out a huge ring of keys and fit one of them into a wire cage against the wall. He got in the cage and started passing me boxes. From the labels I could see they were Christmas lights. Every year, the Inn had a giant Christmas tree shipped down from Canada or someplace up north. Reggie and his workers always dug a big hole in the yard in front of the Inn, and they stuck the tree in the hole like it grew there. Then they decorated it with lights. These must be the lights. From the number of boxes Reggie handed me, I knew we had a shitload of lights.

Then we got in the cart and moved to a different cage. Reggie and I hefted an electric generator onto the cart.

The cart was almost full, but Reggie had one more stop. Way in the back there was a wire cage that looked extra strong. It was different than the others, with wire over the top so you couldn't sneak in from above, and the wire looked like the kind they use in prisons. Reggie used two keys to get in. We loaded in a bunch more boxes. Each one was long and skinny. Maybe they were shovels. The last box was electrical stuff, I could see that. I figured we picked up more Christmas lights.

Finally we were done. Reggie's cart was overloaded and riding low.

We got the big shed doors closed behind us, and Reggie pulled the cart onto the golf course. Behind us, on the other side of the Inn, we heard the band playing.

It was quiet as we motored along. The wind changed and smells from the dinner blew over us. It reminded me that I hadn't eaten much all day.

We pulled up beside the Big Banyan. The top of the tree glowed gold from the sunset but the bottom, where all the roots and vines were, was dark. Reggie whistled low like a bird does at night. Then there were dark figures in front of us, drifting out from inside the tree and circling the cart. I almost bailed out of the cart and ran. Then Reggie called, "You boys, you ready?"

A deep Caribbean voice said, "Hello, Mr. Wolf." A shape stepped forward. It was Jean Claude, the waiter from our breakfast at the Inn.

He slapped me on the shoulder. "Nice to see you again. Did you enjoy our bacon?" And then he laughed a low rumbly laugh, and all the other guys laughed, too.

He turned and talked to everyone else. "OK, gentlemen, let's get these boxes unloaded and the tree decorated."

When the last box of Christmas lights was pulled off the cart and two guys lifted the generator, Reggie got back in the cart, turned the key, and started to back up. I looked up startled, and ran over to him. His cart was still loaded with the skinny boxes. "Wait. Where are you going? What about digging the hole under the tree? How is that going to happen?" I didn't see that Reggie's guys had any shovels or anything. Besides, they were climbing all over the Big Banyan, stringing lights.

Reggie just grinned. Most of the time I loved that grin, but sometimes it really pissed me off. Like right then. "Wait for it, Mon. It'll happen."

"But where are you going?" I know I sounded like a titty-baby. I couldn't help it. Reggie just pointed in the back of the cart. "Boom, boom, Mon." And he drove away.

It was quiet except for the low talk of the guys up in the tree and the sound of the band from back at the Inn. *"Boom, boom?" WTF did that mean?*

I stood there with sweat running into my eyes from under the Rastacap. A mosquito buzzed around my face, and I slapped it on my forehead. I felt something crawling on my leg, and I kicked at it with my foot. I turned on my phone flashlight and stuck it under the bushes under the tree. It looked just like it did before when I crawled under there. Un-diggable.

I heard it before I saw it, a low rumble of a machine coming from the other side of the Big Banyan. I jumped up, ran around the big tree, and looked on the other side. It was some kind of equipment coming across the golf course with two big lights up high, shining on the ground in front of it.

At first I thought it had something to do with the dinner. I mean, who would drive something like that across the golf course in the middle of the night unless they had permission? But it kept getting closer and closer, and then it drove right up to the Banyan. It stopped, but it kept running.

"Hey, Wolf, here's your backhoe. Where should I dig?"

The voice was familiar. I squinted into the lights but couldn't see who it was.

"C'mon, Wolf, tick-tock. Your girlfriend paid me to dig a hole by midnight. I need to haul ass. In case you didn't know it, people think it's suspicious to be doing work on a golf course in the middle of the night."

Minch! It was Jordan Minch. *"Your girlfriend hired me."* I shook my head. Of course she did.

I didn't know where to tell him to dig, so I just pointed. The big shovel thing on the back of the backhoe lifted up and started to turn. A couple of big smashes with that shovel dug a pig-sized hole through the roots of the tree. There was a pile of shells, brush, and dirt next to it.

From up in the tree, Reggie's guys cheered.

Jordan was done and rumbling on his way back across the golf course.

OK. We had the hole.

**8:00 p.m.**

My heart stopped (exaggeration) when I got a text from Sam:

**"Can't find Pinkie in Manatee Hole."**

And then, right after that, a text from T. Rex:

**"Your pig is back in the freezer."**

*Hultz!*

1. T. Rex said she bragged about having a big surprise for me.
2. Sam couldn't find Pinkie in Manatee Hole.
3. Pinkie was back at the shelter.

That bitch.

I tried to think and plan, but all I saw was red.

I thought of Joel's Escalade. T. Rex said it was out in front of the Inn. Then I thought of Joel. He'd be hugely pissed if I took his Escalade again. So what? We weren't going to come this far and lose Pinkie to Hultz again. I just acted. Everything I'd gone to counseling for, down the crapper.

I texted Sam:

**"Going to get P back."**

And then I ran.

When I got out in front of the Inn, I slowed down and tried to catch my breath. There would be people around the cars in the circular driveway. I thought about how I was dressed. Scrub pants from the clinic and the golf shirt with the sheep on it. Running shoes. And the Rastacap. I tried to imagine how some prepster who worked for the Inn would dress. Right away, I took the cap off and stuffed it in my back pocket. I patted down my hair. I couldn't do anything about the scrub pants, but I smoothed them down and tucked in the golf shirt. I held one arm down at my side to hide the rooster scratches and used the other one to hold my phone to my ear.

I walked right into the parking circle. The first person I saw was a tall State Trooper in full uniform, leaning on a big, black Lincoln. *Shit.*

I talked loud enough so he would hear. "The Escalade? Yessir, I'll bring it." Joel's Escalade was blocked in the driveway between the Governor's Lincoln and a red Ferrari.

The Trooper watched me as I made a big show of getting off the call and walking over to the Escalade. I called out to him, "Yeah, emergency, I guess. Bad reaction to shrimp. Anaphylactic shock. Some guy's gotta get his wife to the hospital." I don't know why I said that—big surprise, right? I knew about the shrimp reaction from Discovery, but I miscalculated the Trooper's reaction.

He sprinted for the back of the Lincoln. "I'll get the defibrillator."

*Sweet Jesus. I didn't want him to help. I just wanted him to move his stupid car.*

I called to him, "The guy's pretty embarrassed about it. I don't really think it's the shrimp. His wife's just really drunk already. He wants to get her out of there."

The Trooper stopped, but he looked skeptical.

I thought about what more I could say. "She was talking about a bunch of stuff she wanted to say to the governor. I think we better help her husband get her home."

That got him. He said something under his breath, got in the

Lincoln, and pulled it onto the sidewalk. I got in the Escalade, saw the key on the passenger seat, pushed the start button, and laid a little rubber getting out of there. The first thing I noticed was the rotten boar smell. No wonder Joel was still pissed at me.

Yeah, I know I failed my driver's test three times, but with all that practice, I could drive OK. Anyway, I made it to the shelter in less than ten minutes and blasted the horn when I pulled up to the back door. The door flung open, and I felt like kissing T. Rex. There he was with Pinkie on his big cart. She was all wrinkled and shriveled up from spending the night in the salty Manatee Hole, but it was Pinkie. What other pig had a bullet hole through a star on its forehead?

T. Rex grinned and saluted. "Missing something?"

I popped open the big back gate of the Escalade, and T. Rex rolled the cart up. Together, we got our hands under Pinkie where we could lift and shove. Right away, I realized Pinkie wasn't frozen anymore, she was air temperature. And slimy. I also noticed a big chunk missing from her butt. Shark bait.

"Lift!" I said, and T. Rex grunted.

My hands slipped, but then I got a good hold on a back leg, and Pinkie kind of slurped off the cart and landed halfway into the car. "Again," I shouted, but Pinkie was stuck there. We couldn't get her further in. "That will have to do." I gave T. Rex a fist bump and jumped back in the driver's seat. I heard T. Rex shout something about Hultz as I drove away.

Now I had two new problems. First, my hands were all slippery and I had a hard time with the steering wheel. Second, the back gate of the Escalade was up and that meant the lights inside the car stayed on. I pushed every button on the dashboard I could find, and they stayed on. Every time I went over a bump, the gate plopped down on Pinkie and sprung back up in the air. I saw the whole thing in my rearview mirror.

Right after I went over the bridge from the mainland to the island, I texted Sam (I know, no texting and driving, but it was an emergency).

**"On way with Pinkie. Where to?"**

Right away, I got a response:

**"Leave car on road next to Manatee Hole. You come to**

**dinner. Hurry."**

I skidded to a stop on the street next to the Manatee Hole docks. I still couldn't turn the inside lights off. As fast as I could, I ran around the back of the Escalade and tried shoving Pinkie in further. I didn't want anyone to see her hanging out. No go. She was just too heavy. (Or I was too weak—a definite possibility) I had to stop and lean over with my hands on my knees.

"Hey, Wendell. How's it going?"

I jumped a couple of feet in the air. Right away I recognized his laid-back Southern accent. Sheriff Pruitt leaned against the dock railing, smoking a cigarette.

"Whatcha up to?" He had this big smile on his face.

My first thought was to lie, make up a good story. But Pinkie was hanging out the back of my dad's SUV and the lights were on. Hard to lie about that.

I made a quick decision. I knew Sheriff Pruitt liked Sam. Pruitt helped Sam re-bury the turtle eggs, and I was pretty sure he saw my foot when I was hiding in Sam's cabin and he didn't say anything. Pruitt was a good guy.

"Sam needs Pinkie. We're going to bury her. She told me to leave her here, but now she wants me up at the dinner." The words poured out like a fire hose. It felt a little bit weird, telling the truth.

Pruitt took a drag on his cigarette, then he put it out on the railing. Carefully, he put the dead butt back in the pack. Then, "I better help you push that pig in there. Hultz is all over the place tonight."

I let out a big breath of relief. After we got her shoved in (Pruitt was a lot stronger than T. Rex), he said, "You still here? Better get a move on. Tell Sam I said good luck."

I half-ran and half-limped up the golf course. Even from far away, I heard the music change up at the Inn. Before, the band was playing stupid shit like orchestra versions of Beatles songs. That's the kind of music Joel and my mom and their friends listen to. The music stopped, and then there was just a slow drumbeat.

And a low human voice started, repeating the same words over and over. It was chanting, and I knew exactly what it was.

And then my phone vibrated. It was a text from Sam:

**"Hurry."**

I ran.

**9:30 p.m.**

The chanting was the Calusa Corn Dance song. I knew it because Sam played it over and over in her cabin.

The guests stopped dancing and eating and just looked at each other. They had no idea what was going on. Their Beatles music was replaced by something strange.

I ran up from around the side of the Inn and stopped near the stage, outside the light where people couldn't see me.

I looked at the band. Instead of the five guys in tuxedos I saw before, there were now ten drummers. They each had long black hair and dark skin like Sam. They were all dressed in Calusa vests with beads and shells sewn on. Every one of them had a feather in his hair. They had these big Indian drums tied around their necks with leather straps.

In front of them, there was a tall lady with long braided gray hair. She was dark-skinned like Sam and the drummers. She had on a light colored dress, decorated with shells and beads. In the spotlights, it shimmered. There was something about her that was familiar.

And she chanted the words to the Calusa Corn Dance into the microphone. This must be Sam's surprise. Where did Sam find people to dress up as Calusas?

I was behind the head table, but I could see the line-up. The governor was in the middle. On one side of him was a podium. Joel (wearing a stupid pirate's eye patch) was next to the governor on the other side (of course), and next to him was Pugsley. Next to Pugsley was Mrs. Pugsley. I hadn't seen her since she started this whole thing by slamming into Pinkie with her golf cart. Witch.

The governor nodded his head to the chanting like he knew the tune. What an idiot. It wasn't a Beatles song. Joel whispered in Pugsley's ear and waved his hands around. I could tell Joel was upset, because he was redder than usual. Joel started to stand up, but Pugsley put a hand on his arm and said something. Joel sat back down.

All of a sudden a spotlight from a palm tree lit the chanting woman from behind and she glowed even more. I know she didn't really glow—OK, maybe she did—and the whole thing was pretty weird, but the crowd must have thought it was part of the dinner because they all just sat there and listened. In the dark night with the full moon, the Japanese lanterns, and the quiet drumming and chanting, it was so pretty and so strange.

And then I wondered again. *Where did Sam find these people?*

**10:00 p.m.**

The drumming and the chanting suddenly stopped. There was a tapping on a microphone, and I looked at the head table. The people at the tables looked around, wondering what came next. Except for the crickets and frogs on the golf course, it was totally quiet.

I moved up to the side of the head table so I could see.

*It was Sam at the podium!*

There was a low buzzing noise from the crowd.

Sam was beautiful. First of all, her hair was shiny and black, prettier than I had ever seen it. She had it swirled around on her head with all sorts of feathers stuck in it. It sounds weird, but it wasn't. You had to see it.

She wore something I'd never seen before, this dress made of a soft shimmery material with beads and small shells sewn on it with really complicated designs. This sounds a little strange, too, but on Sam it looked good. The dress didn't have sleeves and Sam had some sort of oil on her dark arms. Her thighs and her legs were all shiny, too. She had moccasins on her feet.

The spotlights from the palm trees made her hair and the oil on her arms shine. The shells and beads on her dress sparkled. Because she was so tall, she looked totally in charge, standing behind the podium with the microphone in her hand. Next to her, the governor looked shrimpy.

"Ladies and gentlemen." Sam spoke in her low voice, then paused and looked around. She smiled, and her teeth were so white against her dark skin. "Governor and other important guests." The stupid governor smiled and waved like he knew what was going on.

"Thank you for inviting me to speak." I saw Mrs. Pugsley whisper something in her husband's ear, and Pugsley shook his head and pulled away. She was really mad. I knew that face from the cart accident. Then Joel whispered something in Pugsley's other ear. He was mad, too. I smiled for the first time. This was going to be great.

"We are here tonight to recognize our Calusa heritage." Next to her the governor nodded, like he thought this was a good idea. All through the crowd, people in their pirate costumes nodded, too. Of course none of them knew what was going on.

"The Calusas were the original settlers of Banyan Island, and recognizing our contributions to its culture is long overdue." I watched the governor think about that for a couple of seconds, and then he nodded his head again. The audience agreed, and everybody nodded.

"So we are here tonight to dedicate the Calusa sacred burial ground under the Big Banyan." I felt myself smile even more. Now I knew what Sam was up to.

Joel yanked on the governor's sleeve and whispered in his ear. The governor shook his head like he didn't understand. Pugsley rose halfway out of his seat.

The audience started to shift around in their chairs. They didn't know how to react. They'd been nodding along with the governor, but now the governor was shaking his head, and this girl dressed up as an Indian said somebody was going to do something to the Big Banyan? I mean, most of the guests were golfers. That big tree in the middle of the golf course was sacred to them, too.

I looked back at Sam to see what she was going to say next, and I saw her texting. Then there was a huge explosion.

**10:15 p.m.**

The sky lit up overhead. It was the fireworks. It took me just a couple of seconds to figure it out. *That's what Reggie had in those long boxes. That's why Reggie said "boom-boom."* Sam must have texted him from the podium.

One by one, they blasted up in the sky.

The dinner crowd stopped wondering what was going on at the

head table and oohed and aahed. This was something they were used to. There were fireworks all the time on Banyan Island for weddings and other stuff, and Reggie was always in charge of setting them off. I should have remembered that.

It went on for fifteen minutes. The wind blew the smoke right over the Inn. Then there was the grand finale with everything going off at once with all the fire and noise. The smoke seemed to settle on the dinner, and I saw people coughing and waving their hands in front of their faces to push it away. Then there was silence.

**10:30 p.m.**

After thirty seconds or so, a little sea breeze came up and you could see a little better, but the whole place still smelled like gunpowder.

At the head table, the podium was empty. Sam was gone. So were the Calusa drummers and the old lady.

Then the chanting and drumming began again. But this time, it was in back of the crowd, in the distance, down by the bayou where the fireworks were set off.

I squinted. There was a glow down there. It wasn't lights exactly, and it wasn't the fireworks. It flickered like a fire, but in the leftover smoky haze, I couldn't see very well.

Then I heard the microphone whistle. It was Joel, and he was up at the podium. "Ladies and gentlemen, I apologize, this isn't a part of our program…."

I couldn't believe it. *Futzing Joel. He was going to ruin everything.*

Whatever Sam was doing, she needed more time.

I knelt down, duck-walked behind the stage, and found the electrical cord to the sound system. It was pretty easy, actually. It was the only cord back there, and it was going to a big console with lights on it. Even a Sped Shed kid could figure that one out.

"I'm the chairman…." Joel's voice on the sound system cut out. He looked around, his face was red and sweaty, and his eye patch was crooked. His big night was going to be ruined. He tapped the mike, but it was dead. So, he just started yelling to the audience. "This isn't a part…."

The audience didn't know what to do. The smoke had cleared, but the microphone was off, the girl in the Indian clothes was gone, and now the drumming and chanting were coming from down by the bayou. And Joel Wolf, a guy most of these people knew, was yelling at them.

I got right behind Joel and boosted myself up onto the stage.

Mrs. Pugsley jumped up, made a move for me, and hissed, "You little prick." (That Mrs. Pugsley has a mouth on her.) But then Hultz surprised both of us when she grunted herself onto the stage in front of Mrs. Pugsley and grabbed my arm. It hurt like a bitch. God, she was strong. I couldn't help it, but I screamed "Owww."

Joel stopped yelling at the audience and looked to see what was happening. He saw it was me. "What are you?…" Sweat ran down his forehead, through his eye patch, and into his eyes. His face looked like a tomato.

I don't know why I did it, but I managed to turn and stuck my hand out to the governor—with the one arm Hultz didn't have in a death-grip.

"Hi, I'm Wendell Wolf. I'm Joel's son. Thank you very much for your support for this Calusa monument. It means a lot to the people of Banyan Island."

It was total bullshit, I knew that. But I sounded like a politician, and I think that's what got the governor. That, and the fact that I was Joel's son. I mean, Joel wouldn't be letting his son do crazy shit, would he?

The governor took my hand. He hesitated at first (I still wore the Rastacap and scrub pants, but I had my white golf shirt tucked in), but when you stick your hand out to a politician they have to take it. It's what they do. I saw Pugsley shake his head at Hultz, and she let go of me. I held on to the governor's hand. He mumbled, "My pleasure (blah, blah, blah)…long overdue…(blah, blah, blah)." You get the picture.

That was all the time we needed. Suddenly, the drums coming toward us were louder. I saw this glow coming across the golf course. The audience all stood up to see better, and some of them started down there. I let go of the governor's hand and ran.

**11:00 p.m.**

Twenty people in Calusa outfits moved slowly up from the bayou. Most of them held torches—they were really tall tree limbs with burning wads of grass tied on them. The gold and orange light from the torches sparkled off the shells and beads of their Calusa outfits. Everybody had feathers in their hair. The torch-carriers formed a lighted, moving rectangle. The wind carried bits of flaming embers up into the sky so the whole thing looked like a burning moving van rolling up the golf course.

The Calusa drummers led the procession, and they still had their tom-toms or whatever they called them around their necks. They were doing a slow march thump-rhythm, the kind you hear at military funerals in the movies. Thump, thump, THUMP. Thump, thump, THUMP. I could see their oiled arms going up and down in unison as their hands hit the leather drums.

The old lady chanter marched just behind the drummers. Her gray hair sparkled yellow in the torchlight. She did this sad, low, moaning chant, and she kept time with the thumping. Ha-*yah*, *ha*-yah, ha-*yah*, *ha*-yah.

Then came the big deal: Pinkie Pie. Sam must have had found the Escalade. Pinkie was stretched out on this platform made of bamboo rods. The platform was in the middle of the moving torch rectangle. There were seven or eight guys, plus Sam, carrying the platform, on their shoulders so Pinkie was way high up in the air.

Pinkie had a shell necklace around her neck, and someone had oiled her up. I didn't say this to anyone, but she looked like she was on her way to a barbeque.

The platform was draped with chains of flowers. Somebody had put a big bouquet to hide the shark bite on her butt.

Sam carried her corner of the platform on her oiled shoulder, and it didn't look heavy at all. I saw her looking at me, and she smiled. I was really happy for her. This was what she wanted.

Even though I wanted to keep watching Sam, my eyes returned to Pinkie, way up high. It was so weird. There was this dead pig that caused this whole thing wearing a necklace and being carried on a platform. *So* weird.

The dinner guests were lined up on both sides of the procession. Flashes from phones went off. People on the island love parades.

**11:30 p.m.**

I ran ahead.

On the other side of the Inn I stopped when I saw another glow, and then I saw it was the Big Banyan, way down on the golf course, all lit up with Christmas lights. The lights made it look huge. It *was* huge, I guess, but the lights made it look even bigger. It looked beautiful all alone out there near the ocean.

When I got there, I found Reggie and a couple of his guys sitting on Reggie's cart. They each were holding a Red Stripe. Reggie had a big smile on his face. "Woo-ee, Wendell-boy. You eva' seen such a show?"

His two buddies laughed and toasted with their beers. "Boom-boom!" one of them shouted.

I gave them a thumb's up, but I don't think it mattered. They were already pretty pleased with themselves, as well as being pretty drunk.

Back up at the Inn, I could see the glowing rectangle of Calusas starting down the golf course toward us. All the dinner guests were walking next to them.

Suddenly I saw car lights coming up from behind the Big Banyan. At first, I thought it was Hultz, making another run at Pinkie, but the governor's limousine pulled up. The governor, Pugsley, Mrs. Pugsley, and Joel got out with the State Trooper.

At that point, I sincerely thought we were screwed.

Reggie and his friends did their best to hide their beer.

Pugsley had a flashlight and he shined it in the hole Jordan had dug under the tree. He shook his head, but he didn't say anything. Joel had his pirate's eye patch on straight and gave me an ugly look with his one eye, but he didn't say anything, either. The governor was the one who spoke.

"Where should I stand?"

I almost laughed. He didn't care about the hole under the Big Banyan or the fact that Sam had hijacked the Heritage Day dinner. He thought this was all planned. The only thing he cared about was where to stand so he'd show up in the pictures.

"Right here, next to the hole," I said, as officially as I could.

**11:45 p.m.**

The torches, the Calusas, Pinkie on her platform, and all the dinner guests got close enough so I could see Sam's face. She was still smiling.

The drummers beat a faster rhythm and the old lady still chanted, but somehow the mood had changed. Instead of a funeral march, it now seemed like a festival or something.

The dinner guests were really into it. A couple of them tried to chant along with the old lady. There was lots of drinking, and people took pictures of the lighted Big Banyan.

I felt a hand on my shoulder. It was Reggie, pointing at the full moon coming up out of the ocean, huge and orange. I checked my phone—*11:57*—we had three minutes to get Pinkie planted.

**11:57 p.m.**

The funeral procession stopped in front of the governor, who stood right where I'd told him to stand. The drummers and the chanter stopped. The Calusas stuck their torches in the ground in a big circle around the tree. There was room for everyone under the tree. After all, it was the BIG Banyan, and it deserved its name.

One of the Pinkie platform carriers made a noise like "huh," and together they set the platform on the ground.

Suddenly there was motion in the Banyan vines behind the governor, and Hultz stepped into the light and said, "You're not going to...."

Pugsley reached out and grabbed her sleeve. He shook his head and said something.

Hultz shut up and faded back into the Banyan. That was it for her.

Sam bent down to straighten Pinkie's shell necklace, and when she stood up, she rubbed her back like it was sore. Then she went to the old lady and put her arm around her shoulders. The two of them walked over and stood beside the governor.

Sam began to speak, her voice low and clear. All the chitter-chatter from the dinner guests stopped as if she'd clicked a switch. The

Christmas lights in the tree, the yellow torches, and the orange full moon made her oily skin shine.

"We are gathered to celebrate the Calusa spirit animal rite of funeral. Leading us will be my grandmother, Kokelus of the Calusa Nation."

I shot Reggie a dagger look. *Sam's grandmother? Her GRANDMOTHER? WTF?*

A million thoughts raced through my mind.

Kokelus spoke in a language I couldn't understand. I caught the name "Nokoomis" once or twice, but that was it. The lame governor nodded along like he understood. At one point he even pulled a handkerchief out of his pocket and wiped his eyes. What a tool.

Sam stood off to one side as Kokelus spoke, and her tears were real. I moved next to her and put my arm around her shoulder. I had to reach up to do it, but I didn't mind. She put her hand on mine.

Now Kokelus chanted lines, and the Calusas, including Sam, responded to each line.

Then the drums started, a different rhythm, slowly. Thump, *thump*. Thump, *thump*. Thump, *thump*.

Several of the platform carriers laid an Indian blanket over Pinkie and tucked it in under her. Then they picked the Pinkie bundle up off the platform and gently lowered it into the hole.

Sam dumped a shovelful of shells and dirt in. She handed the shovel to Kokelus, who did the same. Sam took back the shovel and held it out. The governor reached out for it, but Sam shook her head so no one would see. She handed the shovel to me. I dumped my shovelful in, and I tried to hide my tears.

**12:05 a.m.**

I checked my phone. When the Calusa rules said Pinkie/Nokoomis needed to be buried by midnight, did they mean all the way covered with dirt or just in the hole?

Anyway, it was close. I think we made it.

## The Next Day

I slept with Sam that night. Not "slept" as in "did anything," but slept, as in "slept in Sam's bed." Neither of us knew what to wear, so I took my pants off and she wore a t-shirt.

Sam was warm, and the oil on her skin made her so soft. Her hair smelled like one of those torches, but I didn't say anything about that. We kissed and we hugged. She wanted a back-rub and I gave her one, under her shirt. Somewhere in mid-rub, I fell asleep. Really.

# A Rude Awakening

"Wake up, Wendell."

My eyes snapped open.

Q: *Where was I?*

A: *Sam's voice. Sam's bed.*

"You need to go see your parents. You can't stay away forever." Sam was dressed in her regular clothes, and she leaned into her cabin from the deck. There was sun streaming in from behind her. Then she closed the door, and I felt her steps on the deck above me. The boat rocked as she got off.

*That was it?* I wake up in Sam's bed and she's already dressed and I have to go see Joel? I would have argued, but she was gone. I dropped my head back on Sam's fluffy pillow and thought. I guess she was right. It was time.

I threw off the sheet and stood up. I looked down and saw my underwear and I remembered I'd had them on for the past three days. They were droopy. I tried to remember the night before when we went to bed. Did Sam see my underwear again? That was embarrassing. I got my scrub pants and shoes on, and I stumbled up the stairs onto the deck.

Then I remembered something and went down below and got Reggie's Rastacap. I needed it for courage.

## Facing Joel and My Mom

It was Sunday morning, and Joel didn't play golf until 11:00 a.m. on Sundays, which usually gave him a couple of hours to get over his Saturday night hangover. And if I knew Joel, he'd had a shitload to drink when he got home from that dinner the night before.

He sat at the kitchen table and looked a lot better than I expected. His hair was combed, he was shaved, and there weren't any little shreds of toilet paper on cuts on his face. My mom was at the kitchen counter, humming a Beatles tune. She looked happy, too.

There was even a place for me at the breakfast table. I sat down, expecting the worst. There was the whole Calusa-Heritage Day Dinner thing. And we hadn't talked since my hand accidentally came in contact with Joel's head when he called Sam an Indian slut.

There was silence. I had a few bites of French toast my mom put in front of me, and I was surprised when Joel suddenly wiped his mouth with a napkin and pushed his chair back. I watched him, waiting for the tirade. And then he did something totally weird. He smiled at me.

Up in my room I have a list of all of the expressions Joel uses on me:

1. Grimace
2. Frown
3. Eye roll
4. Puzzled look
5. Head shake
6. "Tick" noise with mouth
7. Sighs/sighing face
8. Angry/red face
9. Crazy circle sign next to his ear
10. And my favorite combo: (while eye rolling and frowning) making a spitting sound with mouth while saying "Russian...."

So, needless to say, I was surprised by the smile.

Then he spoke. "You're grounded for the year." He smiled again. I remember glancing down to see what he was drinking.

I waited. There had to be more. A grounded year was nothing. I was ready to hear words like reform school, social services, or even deportation. Instead: "And I want you to meet with Sheriff Pruitt and discuss the consequences of your actions. I want you to write me a letter listing everything you think you did wrong."

Then he got up and left the kitchen. I think he whistled, "Hey, Jude."

The garage door rumbled up, I heard the Escalade start, then I heard the garage door rumble down.

I gave my mother a question-look, and she shrugged. "The governor personally thanked your father for the Calusa burial ceremony. They talked about making the Inn and the golf course a state historic site. That means the Inn won't pay any taxes. Pugsley congratulated him. He's ecstatic."

I didn't know what to say. *A state historic site, like Granger's? Was I the only one who saw the irony in that?*

I ate a couple of forkfuls of breakfast. My mom whistled "We Can Work It Out" as she loaded dishes.

Could this get any weirder?

I wanted to go see Sam, but first I stopped in my room, took off all my filthy clothes, and took a shower. I sat down on my bed to rest, and I woke up when my phone vibrated at 5 p.m. It was from Sam:

**"Come down to the bayou."**

## I Meet Kokelus

There was an entire Calusa campground right on the golf course, down next to the bayou.

Before yesterday, there's no way the Inn would have let that happen. I guess times changed. There were about twenty tents, not Indian tents, but modern tents from L. L. Bean or someplace like that. In the middle of a circle of tents, there was a big teepee. A real Indian teepee, I guess.

I said *hi* to a couple of the drummers I recognized from the night before, mainly from their long black hair. They were all in shorts and jeans now, and they looked like guys you'd see at a gas station somewhere.

There was a campfire in front of the teepee, and Sam was there with Kokelus. They sat in beach chairs. Sam wore her cut-off jean shorts and a t-shirt, and Kokelus wore jeans and a flowered blouse. They both had feathers in their hair, and they smiled when I walked up. Sam stood.

"Kokelus, I'd like you to meet my boyfriend, Wendell Wolf. Wendell, this is my grandmother, Kokelus. Kokelus is named for the Queen of the Calusas."

Kokelus stood up from her beach chair. She was taller than me, same as Sam, but I couldn't focus on that. Sam had just called me her boyfriend. She'd never done that before. And she said it to her grandmother. Or whoever the old lady was. Whatever, it still felt good.

Kokelus grabbed my shoulders in her hands and kissed me, first on one cheek, then on the other. Then she held me by the shoulders and looked into my eyes. "Thank you, Wendell. Without you, my granddaughter would not have found me."

Right then, I saw how much alike they looked. It wasn't just the fact they were both tall and dark. They looked like a mother and her daughter. Or, a grandmother and her granddaughter. The same eyes, the same smile, even the same gestures. *OK, it might be true.*

## Sunday Night

I slept in my own bed for the first time in three nights. It felt weird.

## I'm a Hero at School, and Some Questions Are Answered

Sam didn't say much on our walk to school, and that was OK, I guessed. I was pretty tired and things were still pretty jumbled in my mind. When we said goodbye at the Sped Shed, Sam said she had to take a make-up test at lunch, and we were having hamburgers with Reggie that night on his boat.

I thought it was going to be hard to go back to school after skipping three days of last week, but it wasn't. The kids in the Sped Shed gave me a standing ovation when I walked in. Word had gotten around about the burial on the golf course, probably from my new Sped Shed BFF, Jordan Minch, who led the applause. I wondered if he was going to ask for more money.

At lunch, Missy Buckler and a couple of the DQs came and sat down next to me. At first I thought they were going to give me some animal rights shit about what happened with Pepe, but they told me how much they respected my commitment to Native American culture. *Right.* I just smiled and nodded and listened. *Whatever.* They were popular, but they sure were stupid.

After lunch, I had a meeting with Mr. Sanders. That's when I first had the idea of using this story as my independent project. (Hi, Mr. S.)

After school I walked home with Sam, and she left me at my house and went to the boat to make dinner. My mom was in the kitchen and Joel was—wait for it—playing golf with Pugsley.

Sam told me the Calusas broke down their campground that morning and went back to the Everglades, so I guess Joel wouldn't have to hit the ball over that teepee.

I told my mom that I was going out with Sam and Reggie, and I waited for her to tell me it was a school night. Instead, she just smiled and said, "You'll have to invite Sam over for dinner here this week."

I just shook my head. Would things ever be the same around here?

We pushed off from Reggie's dock and motored out into the "back-country" islands in the bay.

It was quiet and beautiful, with all sorts of birds flying around and dolphins cruising by.

Reggie anchored in this little cove, but he stayed far enough from shore so the mosquitos wouldn't bite.

Sam set up a card table in the back of Reggie's boat, and she had it all decorated with shells and flowers. She had candles burning in little glass jars. And she looked so beautiful. She had on the shirt she wore to the burial, and it was soft and shiny and the shells sparkled in the candlelight. Her hair was pinned up with a feather, and she had new sand dollar earrings. When she saw me looking at them, she seemed pleased that I noticed and told me they were a gift from Kokelus.

Dinner was my favorite, hamburgers, which Reggie cooked on a charcoal grill hanging off the back of the boat, with tater tots and coleslaw. And Yoo-hoo for me and Red Stripe for Sam and Reggie. And Ring Dings for dessert.

While we ate, we talked about this and that, but we didn't really talk about Pinkie's burial. It seemed like we avoided the dead pig in the room (that's a joke).

After dinner, we didn't talk for a while. Sam and I cleaned up our dishes while Reggie got another beer and tossed the coals from the grill overboard where they sizzled and steamed in the water.

We sat back down, and it was quiet and beautiful.

Finally, Reggie spoke. "So, Sammy-girl, where you take my boat?"

I couldn't wait any longer, so I asked a question, too. "Why did you text me there wasn't any Nokoomis, that the burial was off?"

Sam sat in one of those low beach chairs, and she lifted her head and looked at the sky. The sun was just going down into the ocean. Everything was golden. Then she looked back and sighed. "I was mad. I was sad. I didn't know. I grabbed Reggie's boat and went to the Everglades."

Reggie and I were quiet.

She took a breath, pulled her legs up under her. "OK, I'll tell you the rest. When that asshat Bobby Dash showed up"—she paused and had to clear her throat—"and he told me he might be my father but he didn't want to be my father, I was pissed. But who wants a father like that anyway, right? I mean, his loss." She looked at me, and then at Reggie. I could tell she wanted us to think it didn't bother her, but her voice was tight. "I told him he was an asshat and the least he could do was tell me about his family. I know he was just trying to get rid of me, but the only thing he told me was his family was from a place called Soco Island.

"That was the first I'd ever heard that. I mean, my mom never told me. Why would she? She never wanted to talk about Bobby Dash. I looked up Soco Island on Google Earth, and I couldn't find it. So I got out Reggie's charts and I found it, Soco Island on the Snook River in the Everglades."

She just let that hang there, and we didn't say anything.

"Snook River? Doesn't that ring a bell?" She looked at me and I looked at Reggie and he shrugged. "That was the old myth. There was a secret Calusa settlement in the Everglades on the Snook River."

I shook my head. I mean, Sam told me a lot of shit about the Calusas. Was I supposed to remember every myth?

"Anyway, it was the only thing I could think to do. I took your boat." She looked at Reggie. "Sorry, again, and I went down there. It took me five hours." She paused and took a sip of beer. "I had the charts, so I found the Snook River, but it was Nokoomis who told me to stop at this rickety old dock."

She paused and looked into the sky. The moon was up over the mangroves. Florida may be weird, but it sure is pretty.

"I got out, went up a path, and found this amazing little camp. Over the years, the Calusas found each other and passed on the secret. They come and go, but they always have each other. Kokelus is their leader, and she was waiting for me. Nokoomis told her I was coming."

She stopped and looked at me and then at Reggie, like she wanted us to say we didn't believe her.

There was no way I was going to say anything.

Reggie stood up and went to the cooler for another beer. He

brought a Yoo-hoo back for me and he handed Sam another Red Stripe.

It was quiet for a while, and I couldn't wait any longer. "Did Bobby Dash tell you about Kokelus?"

Now Sam looked up at the moon. I saw tears glisten in her eyes. Now there was a long silence and I let it ride. "No. Nokoomis did."

I sat forward in my chair. Finally, I was going to get to ask all my questions.

I had two big questions. I even numbered them in my mind:

1. "Did Kokelus say Bobby Dash was her son?"
2. "Is Kokelus really your grandmother?"

But I didn't ask those questions. I just sat back in my chair and kept quiet. I didn't know what to believe, but I figured it was enough that Sam believed. I mean, that was Sam being Sam. It was good she believed in stuff

## Monday Night

We tied up at Reggie's dock and left him on his boat. We walked down the marina to Sam's boat. A soft southern wind had come up with all those ocean smells. Little clouds blew across the big moon.

When we got to the picnic table, Sam stopped and put her arms around me and kissed me. We stood there for a long while kissing, and then Sam pulled her lips away from mine and began nibbling on my earlobe. I wanted to laugh because it tickled, but I didn't because it felt so good.

Then I felt a whisper in my ear. I didn't hear it. I felt it on her lips. I thought it was, "Want to stay with me?" But because I *felt* the whisper instead of *heard* the whisper, and because it was such an important question, I just said "Mmm."

With that, she let go of our hug, took my hand, and pulled me toward her boat. I guess I was right about the question. And I guess Sam thought "Mmm" meant "yes."

Later, our heads were on the same pillow and we were awake in her narrow bed and we were sleepy. The candle on Sam's table was almost burned down, but there were still flickers of yellow light on the wooden ceiling.

"Sam?"

"Hmm?"

"If your grandmother was alive, who was Nokoomis?" (I just couldn't help it, I had to ask.)

"Oh Wendell, not now."

Silence.

"I really need to know."

"Nokoomis told you about the burial mounds and when the cremation was. She told me where she was in the Manatee Hole. You should respect that."

"But how could you have a spirit grandmother when your real grandmother was still alive?"

Silence.

"Sam?"

"What, Wendell?"

"Did we really have to bury Pinkie Pie? I mean, that was a lot of work."

"Sweet Jesus, Wolf, sometimes you can be a real titty-baby."

BANYAN ISLAND HIGH SCHOOL

GRADE REPORT

SUBJECT Independent Writing

DATE May 15, 2017

TEACHER'S COMMENTS

Wendell, overall, a fine job! I'm still not sure about the way you camouflaged all your "f-bombs," but this is better, anyway. Good work on the community service. The streets downtown are looking great!

- John Sanders

STUDENT'S COMMENTS

Sweet Jesus, Mr. S! Only an A-??? (just kidding). Anyway, thanks for your help. You're a great teacher!

- Wendell

David Sparks was raised in Illinois and Massachusetts, and now he lives in Maine and Florida. *Burying Pinkie Pie* is his first young-adult novel. He hopes you enjoy reading Wendell's adventure as much as he enjoyed writing it.

David is also the author of the thriller *Built to Fail.* If you'd like to get in touch with David, write him at davidsparks444@gmail.com.